THE DESERT HEART

THE TANESH EMPIRE TRILOGY: BOOK 2

LEAH CUTTER

The Desert Heart
The Tanesh Empire Trilogy: Book 2
Copyright © 2018 Leah Cutter
All rights reserved
Published by Knotted Road Press
www.KnottedRoadPress.com

ISBN: 978-1-943663-78-1

Interior design copyright © 2018 Knotted Road Press http://www.KnottedRoadPress.com

Cover design copyright © 2018 Humbert Glaffo
https://99designs.com/profiles/1756599

Come someplace new…
If you'd like to be notified of new releases, sign up for my newsletter.

I will never spam you or use your email for nefarious purposes. You can also unsubscribe at any time.

http://www.LeahCutter.com/newsletter/

ALSO BY LEAH CUTTER

The Shadow Wars Trilogy

The Raven and the Dancing Tiger

The Guardian Hound

War Among the Crocodiles

The Clockwork Fairy Kingdom Trilogy

The Clockwork Fairy Kingdom

The Maker, the Teacher, and the Monster

The Dwarven Wars

Seattle Trolls Trilogy

The Changeling Troll

The Princess Troll

The Fairy-Bridge Troll

Tanish Empire Trilogy

The Glass Magician

The Desert Heart

The Ghost Dog

Contemporary Fantasy

Siren's Call

The Immortals' War

The Cassie Stories

Poisoned Pearls

MAP

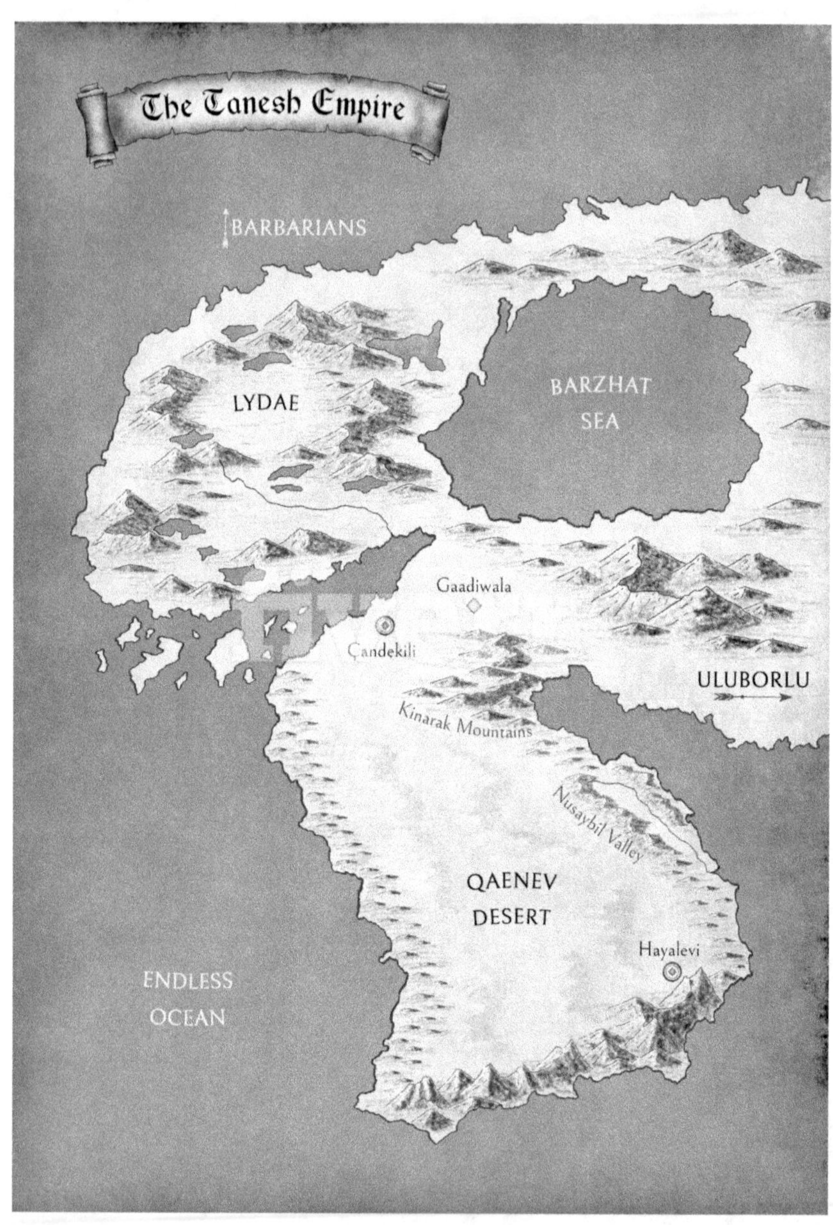
The Tanesh Empire
BARBARIANS
LYDAE
BARZHAT
SEA
Gaadiwala
Çandekili
ULUBORLU
Kinarak Mountains
Nusaybil Valley
QAENEV
DESERT
Hayalevi
ENDLESS
OCEAN

PRONUNCIATION GUIDE

Ç—pronounced as the S in "Sea." TRU-llis (Trulliç)

Zh—pronounced as the S in "Measure." MEER-i-zhah (Myrizhah)

ş—Pronounced as SH. KAR-desh (Kardeş)

ğ—Pronounced with a hard, guttural sound. AH-gkhree-khat (*ağrikat*)

CHAPTER ONE

TRULLIÇ

TRULLIÇ SKIMMED ACROSS THE DESERT, his feet rarely touching the burning sands. He moved as fast as a storm, whirlwinds of sand following in his wake. The white blur of the dog Riyune kept pace with him, staying easily at his side.

Color had burst across the landscape with the rising sun—the peerless blue of the sky and the golden sand that stretched out to all horizons. Trulliç didn't bother teasing out the scents and tastes of every place he passed—the sour, brackish water from a slowly drying up spring, the desiccated remains of a lizard as long as his arm, the taste of iron from the red rocks.

He promised himself that he could come back and explore later. That he would take the time to walk every inch of his newly-discovered home —the great Qaenev desert—and learn all of its secrets and delights.

Anger washed over him. Atça, his mentor and the town wizard of Gaadiwala, had lied to Trulliç. Laughed himself silly when Trulliç had asked if it was possible that the entire desert was his home.

Trulliç would go visit him later and demand answers.

For now, Trulliç needed to get to the southernmost tip of the great desert, to find the foreboding mountains that rose up from the flat land and separated the desert to the north from the endless ocean to the south.

There, he could raise his new city on the foundations of Osmerli, the city of the old kings.

A normal caravan would take months to travel the entire length of Qaenev, and they would have to plan carefully, following the oasis routes when they could, then traveling to the eastern border to continue their journey along the hills there, where they could reliably find water.

Of course, then they'd have to be careful of the slaver ships that plied the coast, catching travelers and ambushing towns unaware.

Trulliç estimated that he would cross the long length of the desert in just three days. Once he'd learned how to pace himself, how to apply his strength correctly, he knew it would take him less than a day. However, during this trip he stopped frequently to sip at streams, to marvel at each and every oasis he discovered, to watch the tiny desert mice hop away from Riyune or elegant, yellow snakes undulate across the dunes.

He discovered that he didn't need to change clothes now. He could wear the same light-weight, gold-and-green striped tunic both in the heat of the day as well as during the colder nights. His plain gray shirt never grew crusted with sweat despite his exertion, his brown wool pants remained comfortable, and sand never bothered his feet in his sturdy leather sandals either.

As he crested another rise and saw the marvelous sands spread out before him, wonder washed away the remains of Trulliç's anger. He'd found his home. The land where his magic was the strongest.

Male wizards, so-called land magicians, were always tied to a particular geographic location. Most had merely a grove of trees, a small pond of water, or even an outcropping of rock. There were ancient tales, of course, of magicians strong enough to affect all trees or all lakes, though they'd only be able to do special magic in their home.

As far as Trulliç knew, no magician had as large of an area as he did to call his own.

The star sisters, on the other hand, could travel everywhere across the Tanesh empire and beyond, and still have the same amount of magic. They were illusionists, not land magicians. Their magic didn't affect the real world, though they certainly could fool anyone into thinking so.

Trulliç felt his heart bursting with joy again. Nadeem, the star sister he'd hired to lead him through the desert, had pointed out the truth to him. Had explained how he belonged in the desert, belonged to the desert, and nowhere else.

What would he have done without her? Would he have survived? Or would he have wandered into the desert, lost and afraid, and let the sands eventually consume him?

He suspected that might be how he died someday—walking into the sands and letting the desert have all of him.

Not yet.

The land changed as he sped along, pure sand giving way to rocks, dirt, and gravel. Scrub now appeared again, thorny plants that only the most hearty of goats or sheep could nibble on. Up ahead, Trulliç felt the edge of his domain, the terribly sharp cliffs with their knife-like edges. Beyond them lay the hateful ocean, the opposite of everything he loved.

He'd seen the ocean once as a child. His mother had thought he was afraid of the waves, that they might carry him away. He had been afraid, but not because he'd thought the waters were out to get him. Rather, it was because they were so alien, wild and constantly moving. The air felt wrong. The sound of the waves grated on his ears. He'd been sickened by the salty smell.

The desert, on the other hand, was still. Peaceful. Quiet.

Trulliç slowed his pace, then slowed further, until he was merely a man again, walking over the sand, not a great magician racing like the wind.

Riyune appeared beside him. He had the same long, pointed snout of a desert dog, though his ears were floppy, not pointed. White fur covered most of his body. Black patches lay across his ribs, too irregular to be called spots. He also had black ears, and smaller black and white spots all along his muzzle.

Only his eyes proclaimed him as something different. They were the same impossible blue as the sky above them.

Trulliç had rarely seen eyes that color before. Traders who came from the northern kingdom of Lydae occasionally had blue eyes. According to his mother, Trulliç's father had had that color of eye, though he'd died before Trulliç had been born.

Nadeem had said that Riyune had a longer, more solid shadow. Under the brilliant desert sun, Trulliç turned to study his constant companion.

He'd once thought Riyune was a ghost, given the odd way he'd first appeared to Trulliç.

However, Trulliç didn't see anything unusual about the dog, who now sat on his butt and scratched his nose with one of his hind legs. Then Riyune stood and shook himself like a normal dog.

Trulliç couldn't help but shiver when Riyune pierced him with those overly bright eyes. Though the dog had only spoken to Trulliç a few times over the years, Trulliç still couldn't help but think that the dog said now: *So? Get on with it.*

"I don't suppose that you could have told me that the entire desert was my home? You know, earlier?" Trulliç asked. Waves of anger crashed over him again.

Riyune didn't bother replying. Instead, he looked at Trulliç, then out over the rocky plain they stood before.

Trulliç sighed. Riyune would likely never answer him. But Trulliç felt certain that the dog had known.

Would Riyune have stopped Trulliç from dying out on the desert sands if he'd gotten lost before he'd found his home?

Trulliç liked to think that was the case. However, he didn't honestly know. Riyune had first appeared to Trulliç as a blood hound. The blood hounds shepherded pregnant women, protecting them if they were carrying a child who had magic.

Was Riyune still just protecting Trulliç until he birthed whatever it was that the dog waited for?

Trulliç would have to ask Nadeem later. She might know about such things, as she was a star sister. And a woman of great power.

He felt connected to her, though he didn't know exactly where she stood on his desert. But he felt certain that he would be able to find her later. Scoop her up and bring her here, to his city.

Trulliç turned to face the open plain. It sat broad and flat, the hills still some distance away, a mere smudge on the flat horizon. Rocks and sand covered the area along with low, green-gray scrub. A quiet squeak from a desert mouse told Trulliç that the nights here would be cooler, probably winds blowing off the far ridge and billowing into the valley.

When the emperor had destroyed Osmerli, the city of the old kings, over two hundred years before, he'd blocked the water that ran from the great Pirazizil river in the east all the way to Osmerli. The oasis trail had run from the border to the city along that constant stream. Nothing taller than calf-high scrub and thorn bushes grew there now, not the tall cottonwoods, palms and figs Trulliç had seen in his dreams.

Nothing remained of the great stream on the plain.

Beneath it, however…

Trulliç pushed his senses under the ground, searching for the ancient riverbed.

There. Right there.

Sand and great stones lay in its path. The banks themselves had been blasted as well, the oasis trail waters no longer able to run true. The ground felt different, not sand but clay and packed earth as well.

Trulliç paused and looked over the great plain. He could *see* the towers he wanted to raise. Tall and square, golden-sand colored, with green and gold banners hanging from every corner. Crenulated walls ran between the towers, and solid guard houses stood underneath. To the west lay a broad market, selling every type of spice and exotic goods.

Sparkling fountains and wells were situated everywhere, so that even the poorest wouldn't have far to walk to fetch water.

With a sigh, Trulliç turned away and started skimming over the sands again, heading toward the Pirazizil river. It would take a caravan at least half a day to travel from the eastern border to Osmerli, but Trulliç knew it wouldn't even take him an hour.

While he could raise the rocks of the city, build a home for travelers and other seekers, what good were fancy buildings and beautiful open courtyards if there wasn't any water?

Trulliç stopped abruptly when he reached the border of the desert. Riyune stopped beside him.

It wasn't obvious to anyone but him, he knew. The land held the same shrubs and scaly thorns on either side. Sand blew constantly from one edge to the other and back. The air smelled the same, full of the musty *meslit* trees and hard-baked earth.

The border cut as sharp as a knife as far as Trulliç was concerned.

He'd only so recently come to the desert. Found his home. Less than four days had passed.

He was loath to leave it again so soon.

Was there another way?

Just beyond the scrublands lay rocky foothills. Trulliç raised his head like Riyune would and sniffed the air.

Did water lay just over those hills? Nestled between those rocks?

He reached out his senses past the desert border. It felt like pushing against wet wool. He could barely see anything, while behind him the desert called to him clearly.

Stubbornly, Trulliç pressed on, forcing his senses underground, seeking the old waterway.

He'd guessed right. The old river did lay amongst the jumble of rocks. It had been diverted by the emperor. Instead of turning to the west and running across the sands, it now turned east.

Huge boulders blocked the old river path, each easily the size of the shack that Trulliç used to share with his mother.

Could he blast them away? Destroy them with his magic?

Possibly. But it would take so much effort. The river ended on land, not in the desert.

Trulliç shook his head when Riyune, who sat next to him, looked up at him with his head cocked to one side, obviously asking what the problem was.

Atça would have pushed the rocks aside. His magic was like that, solid and unyielding.

There had to be another way.

Trulliç walked alongside the border of the desert, heading north, paralleling the river. There had to be some other way to get water to his city. How deep did he have to go to find another river or well?

The first time Trulliç had walked the desert, six years before when he'd been twelve, a secret cavern had shown itself to him. It had contained sweet water. He understood now that all travelers could find this oasis if their need was desperate enough.

And if the cavern judged them worthy.

The cavern had tapped into waters hidden far under the sand, in jeweled caverns. Other travelers had known about the jewels. If they'd gone digging for them, they would have offended the water. It would have left them on the sands to die.

It was always better to be alive than rich.

Could Trulliç just find water near the city site? Could he go deep enough to draw it up?

That didn't feel right. And he couldn't just create water. It had to come from someplace.

The spot where he would raise his city didn't sit on top of a great reservoir.

The water had come from the river. And that river flowed on land that wasn't his.

How could he get access to it without killing what was there? Stealing another man's water was a killing offense.

Trulliç found his feet still walking north, a thread drawing him along. He kept most of his senses pushed underground, seeking something other than sand and rocks. Only a small fraction of his attention watched the golden sands, skirted the scraggly bushes that had recently had their leaves chewed off by a nearby herd of wild goats, felt the solid heat of the sun shining down on the black-and-white checkered *chafiyek* that covered his head and neck and kept the bright light out of his eyes.

Just ahead, Trulliç felt movement. He paused. A dark brown lizard popped up near his feet then scurried over to another hole.

There. A trickle of water coming from the great river. It pooled and died just across the border, in his desert.

The nature of the land there was different. More clay to hold the water in.

Without thinking, Trulliç reached out his senses, then drew back. Ewww. Clay felt slimy against what could be thought of as his magical hands. Sand felt much cleaner.

But sand was also greedy. It drank down whatever water touched it, not allowing it to pool or travel for long distances.

This trickle started in the emperor's lands. But it came to Trulliç's of its own free will.

The emperor couldn't block it without declaring a blood feud or a great war.

Something Trulliç hoped to avoid for as long as possible.

If he went back to where the Pirazizil had been originally diverted and destroyed the rocks there, he'd be tweaking the nose of the emperor. The emperor would be forced to save face and deal with Trulliç immediately.

If, however, Trulliç could tap into an already existing flow of water without affecting those who were downriver…maybe the emperor wouldn't attack him just yet.

Trulliç sunk his senses under the ground again, reaching for the clay.

It didn't respond as well as sand to his touch. Wouldn't stretch and form the pathway he wanted. He couldn't transform the sand to clay either.

Frustrated, Trulliç came back to himself. Riyune sat beside him as if standing guard. That made Trulliç feel better, that no one could attack him while his attention was elsewhere.

It didn't help solve his immediate problem, however.

There had to be some way to divert the stream. Grow it and bring the water to his city.

But how?

Trulliç paced back and forth on his side of the border, growling at the stubbornly uncooperative clay just beneath his feet. The sun had sunk low on the horizon. Already the sand had started releasing its heat. Desert hawks circled above him, twilight hunters looking for any movement they could pounce on.

How was he going to divert the water? He'd followed it upstream a significant distance. A huge reservoir sat under the river. If he tapped into that, then diverted part of the stream, no one would be the wiser. The farmers downstream and to the east of him wouldn't lose their water.

While Trulliç could blast a path through the sand, he needed to start it here. He also realized that just opening up a path through the sand wasn't good enough. He needed to build a riverbank of clay, earth, and rocks so the water wouldn't immediately sink back into the desert.

Trulliç found his fingertips had snuck down, past his waist, to where his glass horseshoe hung.

When his mother Myrizhah had been pregnant with him, she'd bought a tin horseshoe to help ease the birth. However, the tin had burned her belly when she'd placed it on her skin.

The blood hound tending her had magically transformed the tin to glass shot through with ribbons of gold and green, the colors of the old kings.

The horseshoe had always been Trulliç's symbol. It didn't have any great magic in itself. It promised grander things, however. Glass came from heat-blasted sand. Instead of her boy having an affinity toward the metal tin and the tin mines near where his father had come from, he needed to return to the desert instead.

Glass. Trulliç slid his fingers across the smoothness of the horseshoe.

The clay didn't really like him.

But sand—and glass—did.

Trulliç grinned, plucking the horseshoe from its ties.

Why not?

First, he sent a quick prayer to Enkat, the goddess of the rain and water, asking for her help. Then, using two hands and holding the horseshoe like a dowsing rod, with the curve aimed toward the ground, he pushed his will under the earth. He pulled at the remaining heat of the desert behind him, blasting it deep into the sand.

Glass formed in its wake.

The glass seemed thick to Trulliç. Not the sort used in the fancy lamps Atça had had, but instead heavy and impure, studded with dirt and rocks.

Trulliç pushed the glass out until it became a great rounded road under the earth, wide enough for a large caravan to trundle down the center of it.

Then wider still.

It didn't take much for him to encourage the water to start flowing in his direction.

Then he had to race ahead, pushing the glass road along until he reached the old riverbank.

Trulliç paused as he built a curving bank, setting the water to run along the old trail.

The water itself helped him push aside the great boulders blocking the path. The clay came together more easily now, reforming the banks so the river's course would hold true. It grew to about four feet across. Trulliç set his glass road far beneath it, taller than man, so the water would stay cool.

Stars came out, twinkling on the new river. But Trulliç wasn't finished.

He nudged the water along, glassing over some of the worst of the divots in the earth so it would flow smoothly, quickly, into his city.

Long after the moon had set, Trulliç felt all strength flowing out of him. While the sand could bolster him, the water sucked away his magic and power. Plus, he seemed to be more powerful when the sun was up, less so at night.

It was a vulnerability he would have to hide so another magician—or more likely, the emperor—couldn't use it against him.

Trulliç let the water flow into the sands at the edge of the great plain. Tomorrow he would raise the towers and fountains of the city, instruct the water where to flow.

For now, he lay down beside the riverbank, listening to the water gurgle and sing to itself while he dreamed of sand-wrapped blankets and talking stars.

Trulliç woke and stretched. Dawn had cleared the sky of the few clouds that had drifted across the borders. His arms and hands were as sore as if he'd been pushing and hauling barrels of beer all of the previous day. He sat up and rolled his shoulders. They too felt stiff and sore, the coldness of the night having crept into the muscles.

A warm spot pressed against his lower thigh. Riyune lay on his side, still dreaming, his paws making abortive movements.

Trulliç hesitated, then slowly reached down and brushed his fingertips against the top of Riyune's head, sliding them against the soft, warm fur.

The day immediately came into sharper focus. Trulliç sat up straighter, his aches and pains fleeing. The sand took on additional colors, gold and red and even blue hues, while the water turned the blackest black, cold and viscous.

Just past the river, Trulliç saw the ghostly outlines of buildings. Golden square towers boxed in the broad expanse. Toothy walls ran between them. He heard the echoes of long forgotten trumpets and the rumblings of large merchant caravans. The braying of mules and the calling of date sellers. The sweet incense burning to the various altars dedicated to the gods and goddesses: Innis and Serrat, Enkat and Xannil, Onnet and Barzhat.

And a dark altar where no light burned, dedicated to the former goddess Forit. She who'd died to save all that was light from darkness and chaos. Her body fell and became the earth. Her teeth became the mountains, her fingers became the many rivers, the place where her heart had been became the desert.

As the gods and goddesses grieved, their tears fell on her prone body.

Her freckles, the only imperfection about her, became humanity. The darker freckles became the people of the south, the lighter blemishes became the people of the north.

Trulliç blinked and shook his head. The mirage slid away.

So did Riyune, moving apart from Trulliç. The dog stood and stretched like a normal dog would, paws down and butt in the air, before he stretched forward as well.

Where had that vision come from? Had it been the past that Trulliç had just spied? The former city of the great kings?

Or was it a sign of the city to come?

Why had the emperor destroyed the old kings? Was it just so he could take their land?

Or had it been because the old kings wouldn't show the emperor the way to the desert heart? Where Forit's heart still lay, entangled with the darkness and chaos that came before time?

Trulliç, like everyone else, had just assumed the emperor had wanted to take over the kingdom.

Now, he wasn't so certain. Particularly not after seeing the dark altar and the thread of magic that flowed from its blackness.

Riyune wouldn't answer his questions, that much Trulliç knew. Or he'd get the equivalent of an eye roll from the dog.

Sometime, though, Trulliç would need to know.

Trulliç made the decision to start small. Though he felt he could raise a great city, what was the point? No one would live there. Not yet. And the thought of living in a town composed of empty buildings filled him with dread.

Did he call people to him, once he'd built them a place to live? Would they come on their own? He had no idea how that worked. Yerkoyliç had been born in his city, the streets bending to his will as a small child. Atça, as well, had been born in Gaadiwala, the town he controlled.

Since Trulliç could claim the entire desert as his own, he really wasn't certain what to do with the people already living there. He wasn't about to banish them. Or to draw them here, to the city he was raising. Not until there was good trade.

He'd have to figure that out later.

Trulliç took a sip of the cool water from the waiting river. It seemed poised, ready to be directed further. Riyune, too, drank his fill. He'd caught a couple small mice for his breakfast.

Trulliç merely had to breathe in the desert air to be filled. Though he knew he'd miss eating, strictly speaking he didn't need food when he had sands beneath his feet.

And he'd miss tea. That was the first thing he needed to bring here, to…

What was he going to call this place?

Trulliç Town?

He couldn't help the giggle that escaped. No, that wouldn't do.

Trulliç held out his right hand.

Then paused.

It didn't look right. That bare hand raised in the air.

After another moment, he reached down and unstrapped his glass horseshoe again.

There. That looked right. Felt right.

Though he knew the horseshoe by itself had no magic, it appeared to be able to channel his own, give him a tighter focus.

Trulliç raised his hand again, directing it at the flat plain just past the new river.

Stones tumbled together. Then grew larger, as other rocks amalgamated. Stone met stone, squaring off, building higher and higher. The sound of a great sandstorm filled the area. Trulliç tasted the dust in the air. His heart beat hard as the tower assembled itself. He merely directed it. The stones seemed to have a will of their own. They belonged together. Like magnets, they attracted each other. They clanged as they touched, deep booms that reverberated through the open air.

Large openings formed, ready for the glass windows Trulliç would will into place later. The building itself wasn't too wide, maybe thirty feet on a side. A doorway opened at the base. Long slabs of stone flew into the building through the open windows, attaching themselves to the walls as stairs. The top opened and blossomed, forming its own crenellations.

Trembling, Trulliç lowered his hand. He was still tired from his work the night before. Plus, he didn't really want to raise more than one building. Not yet.

He did direct the water to flow over to the black stone he raised for the fountain out front. He shaped it into a pretty circle, three feet around and two feet deep. The water murmured quietly to itself as it swirled. He knew that someone like Atça would have raised a splashing fountain. And maybe Trulliç would do that for other watering holes.

For his own personal well, though, the constant sound of the tinkling water would have been too much of a distraction.

He strapped his horseshoe back to his waist and looked up at the tower. It stood three stories tall, the walls square and true. The color was exactly the same as what he'd seen it in his vision, golden sand that would change as the light did, growing more red with both the sunrise and the sunset, turning a much darker purple at night.

Banners, he knew, would come with time.

And people.

Trulliç walked around the end of the river and toward his tower. It all seemed like a dream.

Maybe that should be the name of the town. Hayalevi. The dream house.

The name floated from him, carried on the winds, up and away, to the edges of his land.

Those who lived in the desert wouldn't have to ask the name of the great city. Its name would live with them, follow them into their dreams.

Would they come to live with him? Trulliç couldn't answer that. But he hoped they might.

Trulliç paused on the threshold of the great tower. The stones he'd raised had gained more mass than he'd realized. The doorway stood a good three feet deep. This would keep the interior much cooler than the exterior.

Did he want to put in an extravagant wooden door? Something he could easily lock? No, that didn't make sense to him. Wood would never become a natural element to him, not something he could work with.

Did Atça have an affinity toward wood? Trulliç doubted it. His former mentor had used a tremendous amount of wood in his house as a sign of wealth, nothing more.

Would Atça had become a stronger magician if he'd surrounded himself with a material that he did manipulate well? That would have sustained him better? Like hard dirt or stone?

Possibly. But that wouldn't have been as grand. Atça needed his ego fed more than his magic.

Trulliç stretched his hand out toward the ground and *pulled* at an ancient rock that he felt buried there. It wasn't the same as the golden walls he'd built. Instead, if felt colder and sharper.

The stone crested the floor, rising only a foot above the dirt there. Then it stopped, stubbornly resisting Trulliç's command.

The black rock looked fragile, with many tiny holes eaten into it. When Trulliç applied a lick of heat to it, the surface smoothed out, becoming like black glass.

Trulliç used both hands and tugged at the rock. Slowly it slid from the earth, rising up to the height of the opening for the door. It stood about two feet inside the tower.

With a wave of his hand, Trulliç set his fire across the entire stone. The divots, pockets, and tiny holes on the surface disappeared. Trulliç felt the rock *settle*. It stood solid and firm, giving him privacy but still allowing people access.

The rock had an awareness to it, alive in a way Trulliç couldn't explain. It would act as a guardian for his door, alerting him whenever someone crossed the threshold.

He didn't know if it would keep an attacker from entering. He had the feeling that it would try to turn away any who meant him harm.

Riyune looked up at Trulliç and nodded, as if he approved.

If Trulliç was being fanciful, as Atça had always accused him of being, he'd say the dog was impressed.

Then Trulliç reminded himself that Atça had been wrong. The things that Trulliç had felt he could do, the magic he wanted to perform, were actually real.

He had to get out of the habit of doubting himself, his abilities.

This was his land. His home.

He was only limited by his imagination and his strength.

He was never going to worry about being *fanciful* again.

With a grin, Trulliç stepped forward, around the guard stone, eager to explore his tower.

His true home.

CHAPTER TWO

NADEEM

NADEEM WOKE IN THE DARK, unsure for the moment where she lay. Cool sand grated against her fingertips, the earth hard against her back. She lay still for a moment, gathering her senses to her. She smelled water—heard it bubbling somewhere close to her left. The air smelled of minerals and old rock, dry but not musty. When she blinked her eyes, she realized that light did enter the space where she lay, a small amount from her right, two long lines, like a lamp shining from behind a tall rock.

It took another moment before Nadeem pushed herself up to sitting. Her left cheek, where her star-sister scar had once proudly been carved, flared with pain. Nadeem closed her eyes for a moment, taking a few deep breaths, forcing herself to ride out the agony and not cry out.

When Nadeem opened her eyes again, she realized she was in a cave of some sort. Rock walls surrounded her. The dirt and sand floor beneath her felt cool, as if it hadn't seen the heat of the day. To her left burbled a tiny stream.

Goddess, she was thirsty. She lurched to her side but thought better of standing. Instead, she crawled to the water.

It felt lukewarm against her skin, not as cold as she'd expected. She brought her wet fingers to her nose. The water didn't smell brackish or bad. Maybe a tinge of iron from the rocks below, but that was it. As her eyes adjusted to the dimness, she realized the tiny stream flowed across the floor of the cave, rising up from just inside the wall to her left, then diving back underground on her right.

Greedily, Nadeem licked her fingers, then cupped her hand and brought more up.

The pain in her cheek suddenly diminished, as though one of her aunts had laid a cool salve over it. Nadeem opened and closed her mouth, testing her limits.

Yes, the pain had greatly gone down. How had the water done that? She wasn't certain she cared—the relief from the constant pain felt too good.

Feeling daring, Nadeem leaned over the stream and splashed water directly onto her wound.

She gasped. The pain hadn't receded that much. Still, as the water dripped down her cheek and across her neck, she felt better. The water healed her, somehow.

Would the wound always physically hurt? That she didn't know. She'd taken her knife and cut through the existing scar on her cheek, then rubbed enchanted sand into it, sand that carried the essence of the desert.

Where was the box? Her knife? Where was she, for that matter? Who'd brought her here?

She found she thought much more clearly now that she'd had some water, the fog from her visions rolling away.

She still wore the same clothes she'd had on before: a long-sleeved, loose, gray-colored blouse to protect her skin from the desert sun, baggy brown trousers instead of a long skirt that most women wore, and a sleeveless tunic, woven with blue-and-black diamond shapes. Her matching *chafiyek* lay on the dirt beside her. Sturdy leather sandals still covered her feet.

In front of her, beyond the small trickle of water, lay horizontal slabs of stone. Like a sleeping place. Or an altar. Rough-hewn rock made up the walls behind the slabs and on either side.

Turning, Nadeem saw the space wasn't very big, maybe ten feet square. Opposite the stream lay the opening to the cave.

Then she blinked.

Was she not awake? Still dreaming?

Slowly, Nadeem crawled toward the opening.

A rock stood just inside the rough stone doorway, blocking the opening while still allowing light and air to pass through.

Just past the doorway stood the open desert. Nadeem had fallen in the scrublands. Not this far onto the sands.

Stars streamed across the night sky, making it as bright as twilight. She couldn't count the number of stars she saw. Watching them fly across the sky that way made her dizzy.

Golden sands spread to the dark horizon. The ground glittered with its own light, as if pieces of glass reflected the shooting stars above it. Nadeem reached a hand across the threshold, scooped up a palm-full of sand, then let it slide out.

She felt every grain of sand against her skin, as if each was alive. It felt cool as well, sending chicken flesh across her shoulders. She shivered.

What was this place?

Nadeem had had visions her entire life, many more since she'd first been marked as a star sister, six years before when she'd been thirteen, at her coming of age ceremony. The *ağrikat* shells rubbed into the open wound had caused her visions to grow deeper and wilder.

This wasn't a vision, however. Nadeem couldn't say how she knew that, just that she did.

But she wasn't actually in the Qaenev desert, either. This felt like an in-between place, neither here or there.

What would happen if she left the comforting enclosure and wandered the desert? What would she find? A way back to the world?

Or an entrance to the realm of the gods?

She didn't know.

The stream called to her, tugging her back further into the shelter. She knew now that it wasn't a cave built into the side of a hill, as she'd first thought. In the morning she'd take a walk all the way around it. It was probably just an outcropping of rocks.

Nadeem drank more of the lukewarm water. It satisfied her as much as a full feast.

When she was finished, she pushed her hand into the water, digging her fingers into the rocky bed.

A vision overcame her, stealing her sight.

Underneath the rocks lay a great, bejeweled cavern. She had the impression that if she dug out just one of those gems, she'd be rich the rest of her days.

But going digging for them would offend the stream, the rocks…this place. It would leave her in the desert itself and let her die of thirst.

Nadeem nodded as she withdrew her hand. Other travelers had used this cavern, called it to them during their greatest need. They also knew of the gems and jewels and had all decided that it was better to be alive than rich.

After another long drink of water, Nadeem pushed herself up to standing. She swayed, every muscle depleted. Why was she so weak? By destroying her star sister scar, had she drained all her strength?

Nadeem listened, listing, as the stream and the rocks told her to go lay down. Regain her strength. Sleep on the stone slabs.

For a moment, Nadeem resisted. She wasn'y going to lie back down on the ground again, damn it!

Then she swayed again, almost falling over.

The cavern had done her no harm so far. She wasn't just being stubborn, but stupid, a fine line that she'd crossed many times before.

Slowly, carefully, Nadeem stepped over the trickle of water and sat down on the bottom slab. It felt wonderfully cool under her fingers. She yawned, then stopped her yawn partway.

Her cheek was no longer on fire. The pain had withered tremendously.

What was this place?

Nadeem didn't know, but she was going to have to ask Trulliç.

If she was ever allowed to leave this place.

<hr>

Nadeem woke as the sun rose, the light creeping around the guard stone that stood in the opening of the cavern. She looked around as the light grew brighter.

The rock wasn't solid. Instead, it looked as though it had grown into walls, the stones merging one into the other. The creek itself stayed the same, just a tiny trickle of water. Nadeem looked more carefully at the stone slab she'd slept on—it was just a plain, irregular, long piece of rock set into the wall. Three others lay stacked above her. It would be easy to climb from the bottom to the top.

She nearly giggled at the thought. The place slept four, but no more.

Stretching, Nadeem's muscles in her arms and back pulled, still slightly sore, as if she'd climbed and fought a lot the day before.

And maybe she had.

Nadeem swallowed against the bile that had suddenly filled her throat.

Before she'd gotten to the cavern, or it had come to her, she'd been lost in her visions.

The vision told of endless war. The black gibbering darkness of her dream place had been loosened on the earth. The very gods themselves fought it, while the emperor had been corrupted and fought against them, spreading filth.

She'd fought long and hard beside two-faced goddess Barzhat, the goddess of death. Each of the goddess's twelve arms held a long knife, and her four legs danced as she killed all who came upon her. Both her blue face and her black face cried golden tears that turned into the weights the dead wore.

But even the goddess couldn't hold out against the darkness.

Nadeem had had to kill Barzhat after she'd been corrupted. The fight had been to the death of both parties though, and Nadeem had fallen a long, long time, as long as it took for a star to fall from the sky into an endless pit.

Nadeem shivered. That hadn't been her only vision after she'd removed her star sister sign. But that one had been the most powerful.

With trembling fingers, Nadeem reached up and touched her cheek. The skin felt rough, the edges of her scarring apparent. It was sensitive, too, sore like it was bruised.

Slowly, Nadeem made herself stand. She stretched. Yes, her muscles still hurt, but it was a good ache that showed she was recovering. She bent over and touched her toes, then did a few more stretches in place.

She wasn't up to full strength, that much she knew. She was still recovering from…something.

She took another step and knelt by the water. Two mouthfuls made her mind clearer.

She stared at the water. It wasn't magical. She couldn't see any hint of magic flowing through it.

Yet, it was still special.

Nadeem walked over to the opening looking out over the desert. The foothills weren't that far away. She was possibly only half a day's walk to the scrublands.

How had she gotten here?

Now she saw that her pack had come with her. It sat next to the opening of the door. Had it been there the previous night and she'd just missed it? Possibly.

Or possibly not. She hadn't been in the actual desert the night before.

She eagerly tore into one of her travel rolls made of crushed walnuts, cracked wheat, chopped figs, and held together with *meslit* syrup and a paste made of dates.

Only after she'd finished eating (and had drunk her fill of the sweet water) did she do an accounting of her belongings.

The magical box that had held the essence of the desert in its enclosed sands—the land box, as Trulliç had called it—was no longer with her.

Same for the cane she'd carried from Koruli. She'd been sent there to kill Malik, her first assignment as one of the star sisters who reported directly to the emperor and did jobs for him.

She'd failed that task miserably. One of her former teammates had killed Malik instead, and they'd had to burn down the house to hide the evidence so the death would appear to be natural.

Nadeem still wondered if by killing Malik they'd killed the entire town of Koruli, turned it into a slave camp for the emperor.

Malik had received the fancy walking stick as a gift from the emperor himself. Fine black wood made up the base of it, while the top of it held a silver head in the form of a snake.

Nadeem had taken it with her, casting a heavy illusion on it so that it would appear to be a stout walking stick.

Where had the box and the stick gone?

Nadeem wasn't sorry that the land box had disappeared. She had a feeling that Trulliç would find it and use it.

The stick though….It wasn't magical, not like herself or Trulliç. There was still something to it, something that wasn't quite right.

When she got to the foothills, she'd have to backtrack and see if she could find it.

From the position of the sun, Nadeem knew the outcrop of rocks faced directly west. She debated leaving at that point, walking to the foothills.

But she knew that though they didn't seem that far away, it would take hours to reach them. No one traveled in the direct heat of the day in the desert. Except madmen and fools.

Nadeem, for all her mistakes, still wasn't a fool.

She walked back to the water, taking another long drink as well as filling her own water skins.

Then she laid back down on the bottom most slab and napped, recovering her strength.

She had a feeling she'd need it.

With twilight came gentle breezes, licking Nadeem's scarred cheek. It still hurt but not nearly as much as it had. A ghost of pain to remind her of what she'd done.

At some point she'd have to find a mirror to see what she now looked like. She'd attempted to disfigure the star that had been carved by Aunt Parayat at her coming of age ceremony. She knew she'd managed at least a few long cuts bisecting the existing lines. Then she'd tried to carve a curving line through the mess as well, though her hand was shaking so much at that point she wasn't sure how well she'd succeeded.

Nadeem took one last long drink of water from the tiny stream. Then she bowed her head and thanked it for its hospitality, as if it had been the most generous host.

And in some ways, that was exactly what had happened.

She also sent a quick prayer to Serrat/Serril, the two-faced god/goddess of desolate places and the primary goddess of the star sisters. She didn't know who else to pray to besides Barzhat, the goddess of death, who was also beloved by the star sisters.

Nadeem couldn't call herself a star sister anymore, however. She'd disfigured the star on her cheek.

She would have to figure out who she should pray to. Maybe Enkat, the goddess of rain. Except that her bountiful curves and the way she let her husband Xannil hide her away, had never sat well with Nadeem.

Maybe she should start praying to Onnet. Yes, she was the goddess of childbirth. She was also the goddess of the hunt.

But who or what did Nadeem hunt? What was she going to do once she left the desert?

Aunt Parayat had been her initial mentor and had taught Nadeem to question everything, even the emperor himself.

Nadeem decided that she would travel to Kardeş, the hidden oasis of the star sisters, and demand answers from her aunt this time, not more questions.

But first, she had to make it out of the desert.

Nadeem knew that as soon as she set foot on the sand, Trulliç would know where she stood. It was probably the only reason why he hadn't already come to fetch her—because she still was in that in-between place.

She knew she couldn't hide from the desert magician forever.

She just had no idea how to face him. How to face her failure. He would remind her of everything she'd lost.

No, not yet. She couldn't see him, not yet.

Still, Nadeem couldn't stay in this place forever. The stream was an incredibly polite host and wasn't making her feel as though she had to leave quickly.

But a good guest didn't overstay her welcome.

Sitting beside Nadeem's pack she found her belt with its traditional three knives, along with the other weapons she generally carried. Without thinking she strapped her equipment back on, all her knives, her blowgun and darts, even a long *meslit* thorn. She hadn't felt naked without her weapons, but she felt better carrying them again.

Nadeem shouldered her pack. Its comfortable, familiar weight made her feel better, even if she hadn't regained her full strength yet. She wouldn't be able to run for half a day with her pack on flat ground, not yet.

It was only a matter of time before she did, though.

Nadeem stuck her head out of the shelter and looked again at the scrublands to her right. Would Trulliç come after her right away? Maybe. Maybe not. It would depend on how much work it would take him to raise his city.

Not very much, she suspected. Then he would come looking for her.

"Thank you again," Nadeem said over her shoulder to the stream. Then she stepped outside onto the sands.

Cool night winds swirled up, then died back down. The stars were just starting to peak out from the dark sky. Nadeem turned first to her right, intending to walk all the way around the outcropping of rock.

From the outside, the rocks still appeared to be grown together, one place on top of another, in tall spires. But no gap lay between each segment.

Malik's cane leaned against the wall about halfway down the northern wall of the cavern. Nadeem couldn't have seen it from the front entrance.

Why was it there? Why hadn't it appeared beside her pack? She was certain it had been tied to her pack earlier—she'd found the straps.

Gingerly, Nadeem reached for the walking stick, as if the snake head might suddenly come alive and bite her.

The wood of the cane felt slippery against her palm, as if it had been greased with pig fat. She'd never seen anything magical about the stick, but she'd known that it was special. Different.

Now, it felt like it belonged in that in-between place she'd just left.

However, the stream had not welcomed it. If she had to guess, she would say that it barely suffered the cane's continued existence. It hadn't destroyed the cane because she had been the one carrying it.

Why was the cane so offensive?

Nadeem set the tip down beside her, probing the sand.

She hadn't left a solid footprint behind her. The sand around the outcropping of rock wasn't that soft.

However, what little mark she'd made as she'd walked disappeared, as if the cane sucked away all traces of her.

Curious, Nadeem took two more steps out, away from the outcropping of rock. Then she deliberately poked at the footprints she'd left behind in the softer sand.

They disappeared.

Nadeem had wanted to get out of the desert so she didn't have to face Trulliç. As the magician of the great Qaenev desert, he'd be able to find her anytime she set a foot on the sands.

With the cane, she could walk the desert freely.

What was the cane, exactly? How did it erase her steps? Why did that offend the stream and the cavern so much?

Questions and more questions.

Would Aunt Parayat provide Nadeem with any answers?

Nadeem hoped to. For her aunt's sake. Because Nadeem's knife was sharp, and she wouldn't hesitate to use it if it put her at an advantage.

Nadeem took a deep breath when she passed over the border of the desert and onto the true scrubland.

Normally, the border was indistinct. The same thorny bushes with scraggly leaves grew on both sides. Sand mixed freely with dirt. Winds blew this way and that.

However, Nadeem could tell. She suspected the border wasn't as distinct for her as it was for Trulliç. He'd know exactly where the edges of his land ran.

But now, she had more of an affinity toward the desert as well. Her mangled cheek told her, if nothing else. Pain stabbed her anew as soon as she stepped over. Not the debilitating pain of before, though she suspected even this ache would lessen.

It would never go away. Not until she placed her feet solidly on warm sand again.

To be safe, Nadeem still walked a ways north of the border. She didn't want to make it easy for Trulliç to find her.

The cane in her hands didn't change once it left the desert. The wood still felt greasy, and the silver head remained cold against her palm.

Now that she was off the sands, however, Nadeem cast a heavy illusion on the cane, making it appear as a stout walking stick. She *blurred* her own features, too. She couldn't make herself invisible—none of the star sisters had that ability. She could make it difficult for the eye to track her. With this disguise, she could walk directly by a man and he wouldn't notice her.

Nadeem looked carefully at her outstretched hands as the edges grew indistinct.

Then they turned darker. She became more like a shadow.

Nadeem stiffened. She'd never had that ability before. Did it come from the desert sand she'd rubbed into her mangled wound?

Had she picked up some of Trulliç's abilities? The power of the sands?

None of the star sisters could cast magic like the land-based magicians. All her magic was illusionary. Though she had been one of the strongest illusionists in her *kabal* of star sisters, she'd never heard of one having the power to become a true shadow.

Had she gotten stronger still?

Gleefully, Nadeem started to run across the scrub. She knew she didn't have the strength to go miles and miles at this speed, not with a full pack. She still felt tired from her visions and trials.

But life wasn't all about revenge, unanswered questions, and pain.

There was still joy to be found, too.

Nadeem stayed in the shadows and carefully counted the number of horses and camels the caravan traveled with. She wouldn't steal from a caravan that needed all of its pack animals.

However, several of these went unburdened and had stayed so for the last two days. She assumed that meant the animals were going to the large market in the next town to be sold.

She'd also heard the men's whispers at night, around the fire, of the new magician and how the desert had come alive, aware in a way it had never been before.

Hayalevi. The town the desert magician had called forth.

Nadeem wasn't certain how many days had passed while she'd been in that in-between place in the cavern. Maybe a week had gone by since she'd last seen Trulliç.

He'd claimed the entire desert as his own, though. And that included any and all who lived in the desert. They shared his dreams, though she did not, protected by the emperor's cane.

While not everyone in the caravan wanted to travel the length of the Qaenev desert, the leader of the caravan had already made up his mind to go to this new place. He bragged about making (yet another) fortune there.

In the meanwhile, Nadeem planned on "buying" one of his animals. Though she could walk and run all the way to Kardeş, going overland on camel would be easier and quicker.

She'd spent time sitting quietly with the animals the previous evening.

They had seemed to accept her, smelling her presence though they couldn't really see her.

She'd never steal from a caravan, not even one as well outfitted as this one. Never take food from someone else's plate. You never knew when you might become the beggar, asking for another's forbearance. Though other star sisters might cheat an unpleasant inn keeper or tavern host, that had never sat well with Nadeem.

She had coin. She could pay.

The defenses around the camp were laughable. The two guards they'd set weren't trained, and though they did stay awake all night, they didn't regularly walk the perimeter.

Did the merchants trust that no one would rob such a large caravan as theirs? Or did they think the animals, themselves, would set up an alarm if a stranger drew near?

She walked between the animals, looking for the one who would carry her without question. One of the male camels had caught her eye—he was young and had great strength. He also seemed more lazy though, and would require a firm hand.

One of the females might be a better match for her. The camel she had in mind had a sweet temper—well, sweet enough for a camel. She wouldn't be as strong as the male or go as long. But she wouldn't need so much minding, either.

Nadeem started walking between the male and the female camels, still unable to decide.

She froze when the leader of the caravan left the main fire and walked over to the horses. He murmured in the ear of the first horse, then stroked the mane of the second, also talking to it.

What was he saying? He appeared to be talking to each of them.

Nadeem waited until his back was turned before she moved closer, confident in her disguise. The man wouldn't be able to see her directly, not as indistinct as her magic made her. Plus, she had added more shadow to her skin, blending further into the night.

"Tomorrow you'll find a fair hand to guide you," the man assured the mare he currently stood next to. "Maybe a farmer who will let you walk his fields." Then he moved to the next mare. "And you! You will have a handsome stud or two, already lined up. Now, don't be bashful. You'll have beautiful colts, strong and mild-tempered."

Nadeem smiled. He seemed to know each of the animals and had already figured out his sales pitch for them.

"And you," he added as he turned.

Who was he addressing? He appeared to be facing the darkness.

"The stranger who visits my crew in the night and makes my charges uneasy. Come out of the dark and be an honored guest at my fire."

Nadeem grew very still. He obviously couldn't see her. He directed his speech to a blank spot in front of him while she stood a few feet to his left. She breathed very shallowly, willing him not to notice where she was.

After a few moments, the man added, "My men think you're a ghost who's come to haunt us. I think you're flesh and blood. Come and sit by our fire, so that I might win some bets." He grinned. "I'll even share the payout with you."

Nadeem kept herself under strict control, not moving, barely breathing, though a smile threatened to break out.

The merchant intrigued her. He would be considered handsome by most, with a tall, broad forehead, a large, hooked nose, and eyes that twinkled with intelligence. His skin was darker than most, though his lips and the palms of his hands were pink. He wore a finely made sleeveless tunic, slit down the center in the southern style, and belted over loose trousers, a plain shirt, and solid sandals.

After a few more moments, he shrugged. "Or don't. Stay in your shadows, play your games. Just don't hurt my horses or camels. They will fetch a nice price at the market tomorrow."

With that, the man turned and marched back to the main fire, his back tall and proud, unafraid of whoever stood behind him.

Nadeem waited, counting her heartbeats.

Should she go up to the man's fire, as he'd asked? Appear in the light and demand to be treated as an honored guest?

He couldn't hurt her. None of them could. She was almost back up to her full strength and speed.

Why not take advantage of his offer? She could always disappear anytime she wanted to.

Besides, she had planned on buying one of his animals, leaving coins behind.

May as well do the bargaining face to face.

With a grin, Nadeem stepped away from the animals. She kept her illusions up around her until she reached the edge of the firelight.

No one noticed her. She was pleased at how well her magic hid her.

Then she stepped forward, dropping the threads of her magic as she came into the light.

The men around the fire gasped. A couple rose, reaching for their weapons. The head of the caravan waved them back down.

"Greetings, honored guest," he said as he stood. "I am Levent. Be welcome at our fire."

"Thank you," Nadeem said, taking another step forward. "I am Nadeem, a traveler of the desert."

The men closest to her, on her left side, seemed perplexed, but they waited for Levent's word. Good. They were as well-behaved as she'd thought.

"Not a star sister?" Levent asked, curious.

Nadeem turned her mangled cheek toward him. "Not any longer," she said firmly.

That shocked the entire crew.

No woman that Nadeem had ever heard about had turned her back on the rest of the star sisters. She didn't know if that put a price on her head or not. She wouldn't be surprised if it had.

"I see," Levent said eventually. He nodded to himself, then continued. "You are welcome as an honored guest," he said firmly, addressing the crew around the fire as much as her. "We will share water, food, fire, and shelter with you," he added, using the traditional phrase.

Then he paused and grinned at her. "Though you've caused me to lose some of my bets, traveler."

He put an emphasis on that last word.

Nadeem nodded. He'd probably bet that she was a star sister.

"Perhaps you have something of interest for me to buy, merchant," Nadeem said. "After we share fire, water, and food."

She had always been planning on buying a travel animal from him.

"It will be my pleasure," Levent assured her. "Please, come, sit beside me and tell me your tales, so that I might learn."

"Gladly," Nadeem said, walking around the fire to the honored spot next to him. A servant appeared out of the dark and placed a clean rug on the ground, along with a new pillow.

Nadeem nodded in thanks, then sat with the rest of the men. Only now did she realize how hard her heart pounded and how dry her mouth had gotten.

They were just men. She could handle them.

But she was no longer a star sister. Had declared herself merely a traveler.

At least they'd seemed to accept her.

Levent clapped his hands. "Food! And water for our honored guest!" he called out.

There would be no stories, no talk or bargaining, until his guest was properly taken care of. Levent was taking his responsibilities as a host seriously.

But then, there would be many questions they would ask. Only some of which she would answer.

For a moment, she regretted her decision to come and sit at the fire.

Levent smiled warmly at her. He was curious, handsome, and intelligent. He'd work to make sure his guest stayed at ease.

Maybe it would all right.

CHAPTER THREE

TRULLIÇ

Trulliç raised his glass horseshoe to the next opening on the second story of his tower. Sand swirled up. The heat blasted his front, making him grin, as the sand solidified into clear, thick glass. It partitioned itself so the bottom section easily slid away, letting the breezes in.

Trulliç laughed with delight. This was how magic was supposed to be! Easy, clean, and joyous.

He took a deep breath, trying to let go of the anger that kept rising. Atça had lied to him, many times over. His former mentor had insisted that magic must be *taught*, that it wasn't a natural ability. That Trulliç could never trust his senses when it came to magic. That Trulliç was being *fanciful* whenever he thought he had some magical abilities.

Soon, Trulliç would go and demand answers from his former mentor.

And a reckoning.

For now, he had one more story of his tower to explore.

He'd kept the first floor as a mostly open space where he could greet people and hold meetings. He stubbornly pushed away the small voice that questioned who he would meet with. People would come to Hayalevi. He was certain of it.

He wasn't destined to live all alone in a great city on the edge of the desert, like some hero from a tragedy.

On the second floor, Trulliç had added additional walls, dividing the space so that guests would be comfortable there.

The stone stairs leading up to the third floor looked the same as the first set—made of long slabs of irregular rock. They reminded him of the pieces of stone that he'd seen in the cavern that had shared its water with him, so long ago, during his manhood journey. The gray rocks had wear patterns on them, as if they'd sat under dripping water for decades. They still held his weight firmly as he stepped up them and through the hole leading to the top floor.

It smelled differently up here. Trulliç paused before he took the final step onto the floor. What was it?

A sweet spice teased his senses. Cinnamon, maybe? Or figs, perhaps?

Trulliç took the final step up.

It was the sweet smell of the desert, her song made into perfume. It lifted his spirits, banished the rest of his anger. Whatever power he'd used that morning was instantly replenished. Actually, he felt stronger now than he had when he'd first woken.

A box sat in the corner of the room.

Even before he reached it, Trulliç identified it.

It was the land box, the box that had been with Nadeem. The box that held enchanted desert sand that Yerkoyliç had created to aid his search of the desert heart.

The box itself was nothing special. Plain wood stained a dark brown, though well made, with interlocking corners. It was perhaps ten inches along each side, and maybe a foot deep.

How had Yerkoyliç made it? Atça had said the land boxes were forbidden. They gave a magician too much power.

Trulliç believed it.

Magicians were land based. Once they left their home, their power diminished.

With a land box, however, a magician could carry a bit of their home with them. Keep themselves strong.

Maybe even challenge the emperor.

The great *Padisha-i-Ghazi* was famous for the long cloak he wore. Each scale in the cloak had been fashioned from the afterbirth of a magician or star sister. Someone with power couldn't fight their own blood. Thus, the emperor protected himself from those who could possibly be stronger than he was.

However, if a group of magicians attacked, and each with a land box…

Trulliç shook his head and pushed those thoughts to the side. The emperor would hopefully accept Trulliç, his power, and his land. Trulliç didn't want to fight the emperor.

Hopefully, the emperor would feel the same way about Trulliç.

Trulliç reached a hand into the box, letting the glowing sands slide through his fingers. He'd originally planned on bringing the sands to the desert and releasing them from their bonds.

Now, he wasn't sure.

The sand didn't feel trapped or constrained. It didn't mind being where it was, sitting in a box away from the rest of the desert. It had more awareness than the rest of the land. Trulliç wasn't certain what exactly he could do with the sand in the land box.

He'd have to experiment and see.

Trulliç paused for a moment. Why was the box here? Where was Nadeem? He couldn't feel her.

She'd left the desert. Though she'd said she'd stay and wait for him.

Trulliç snorted. No, she wouldn't wait. Nadeem didn't *wait* well. He'd only known her for a very short time, but he knew that patience wasn't her strong suit. And it had been, what, a week or more, since he'd left her.

Where had she gone? Not back to Kardeş, the oasis of the star sisters. He'd know if she walked on the desert.

She would come back to him. She had to. He had to reward her, thank her for..well, everything.

Trulliç turned away from the land box and looked over the third floor. He only built a few walls, dividing the space, leaving most of the entire floor open. This would be his study, where he slept and dreamed.

There was one more floor to explore, however. A much smaller staircase led to the roof. The stones there were more like bricks, baked and regular.

From the top of his tower, Trulliç felt as though he could see everything. To the south lay foothills that gave way quickly to the forbidding mountains that guarded his realm from the endless oceans.

To the east lay the closest water as well as the nearest oasis trail. Just past the border in that direction lay towns and people—the emperor's people, but people nonetheless.

To the west lay a lot of desert before the hills began again. More oasis trails curved there, following rivers that still ran in the heat of the summer.

And to the north—sand and more sand. Most of the desert filled that direction, going to the horizon.

Which direction would the people of his city come from?

Trulliç didn't know. But he'd come up here every day to see if he could spot anyone coming.

<hr>

Trulliç spent much of his time in his tower. He didn't want to add banners, not yet. Though he'd seen what they'd looked like before, when this had been the city of the old kings.

He knew his banners would be the same colors, with thin stripes of green and gold. Like the ribbons of color that made up his glass horseshoe.

But there wasn't really much else for him to do here. Not until some other people came.

He'd already planned out where the streets would to. How the fountains would be laid out. The smaller alleys for those who felt they needed to hide. The wide-open markets.

When Trulliç walked across the flat plain, he could see all the buildings in his mind. Riyune walked beside him sometimes. Other times, the dog went off on his own to follow an interesting scent, or to pluck a hidden mouse or small lizard from the dirt to snack on.

Everyday, Trulliç found himself wandering back to his tower as the sun climbed directly overhead in order to go rest in the shade. No one traveled during the heat of the day.

However, Trulliç didn't feel the heat as he once had. It baked his bones, making him feel loose and alive, but he no longer sweat like he had. He didn't really need to hide in the shade like most people else did.

Again, the wash of anger over the lies Atça had told him.

Agitated, Trulliç paced his room in his tower.

What should he do? He knew he should go walk around the

boundary of his territory, the entire desert. He wasn't sure how he needed to strengthen it, just that he needed to. And he'd promised himself more adventures, to go walk every inch of sand and learn about all the life hidden there.

What he really wanted, though, was people. Someone to talk with. How long had it been since he'd spoke to someone? A week? Two?

Trulliç sighed and sat in the center of his room. When he'd been on his first manhood journey, that had been one of his fears. That he'd be stuck living in the desert without any people, only occasional travelers to keep him company.

Riyune nudged his leg.

"I know you're here, but I'm sorry, you're not enough," Trulliç explained. Unless the dog was suddenly willing to talk with him?

But Riyune gave him the dog equivalent of an eye roll before he deliberately walked over to the western window.

"What, do you see something?" Trulliç asked. He eagerly jumped to his feet and looked out.

He couldn't see anyone coming.

Trulliç sent his senses out, feeling his way. No one walked across the desert to come greet him.

However…

An oasis sat tucked away just this side of the western mountains.

A permanent oasis. One that had a small village enclosed inside of it.

Trulliç grinned.

So maybe no one had been able to get to his grand city yet.

That didn't mean he couldn't go visit the people of his land. He didn't have to wait until they came to him.

He could go to them.

Before Trulliç left, he raised one more small building. It stood solid and separate. Just a square room with a guard stone. He left the inside dark and shaded, a resting place for travelers.

In it, Trulliç built two altars.

The first was an altar to Serrat. He'd always been the god that Trulliç prayed to. He was the god who'd brought magic to mankind so he could win a bet with the goddess Onnet. He'd been banished from the land of the gods as a result, and was considered the god of desolate places, like the desert and craggy mountain peaks.

Trulliç dedicated the second altar to Serril, Serrat's female side. The god was frequently represented with two faces—one female, one male. In stories Trulliç had learned as a child, the god could take on either form, and appear as either a man or a woman.

Serril had given birth to the star sisters. She had a birthmark in the shape of a star on her left cheek, which was why the star sisters marked themselves the same way.

The first altar, Trulliç colored the stones black, so people would know it belonged to Serrat. The second, he made the stones white.

But what should Trulliç offer his god? To both aspects of him?

Trulliç reached down to the sand beneath him and lifted up a handful. Then he compressed it with his other hand, as if the sand were clay. Trulliç sang a song of thanksgiving as he pressed the sand together harder and harder. The heat that rose from between his cupped hands refreshed him, drying out his skin.

When he released his hands, a small glass ball floated in the air before him. The glass was black and smooth, like a pearl from the Barzhat Sea. He sent it to sit on the altar for Serrat.

Then Trulliç did the same for Serril, forming a small white glass ball and setting it on her altar.

The glass balls didn't glow, which Trulliç found disappointing. What had he done wrong? They should be a light to all who came into this tiny temple.

When he took a step back, he realized they didn't need to glow.

The sand underneath both altars glowed—a soft, golden light—while the glass balls loomed, protecting the altars.

Whoever came here to pray would automatically recognize this as a holy place. Maybe sometime a priest would come and properly sanctify the altars, though given how the space felt, that might be unnecessary.

Only after Trulliç left the small temple did he realize that he'd broken one of the emperor's recent commandments. Any new building needed to have a small scale-like shape added to its foundation to represent the emperor. Many new buildings were now dedicated to the emperor.

Trulliç reached his hand out to form the shape in the wall of the temple, then drew it back.

Yerkoyliç had claimed that all the recent proclamations from the emperor were because he planned on becoming a god.

People now thanked the emperor at every meal, as if he was responsible for the bounty they were about to enjoy. New buildings had to bear his mark. Bells in the morning rang in his honor.

Trulliç walked away before he despoiled the temple to Serrat/Serril with the sign of the emperor.

This was *Trulliç's* land. His territory. Yes, in the grand scheme of things, it was part of the empire as well.

But Trulliç wasn't about to deface his property with another man's mark.

Not until guards arrived and told him that he must.

The village of Ishmirli held maybe thirty families, so about one third of the size of Gaadiwala, where Trulliç had grown up. They were mostly shepherds or traders, tending the caravans which came through, either on their way to the coast or coming from there. The village had a single inn located in the north-east corner of the tiny market square.

Though Trulliç could have sped across the sands and arrived there well before sunset, he took his time gliding over the land, paying attention to the life he encountered—the nests of mice, the skittering lizards, the desert hawks and smaller birds.

He also marked the edge of his border, where the desert ended and the foothills of the mountains began.

He didn't feel the need to defend that border. First, someone would have to sail the endless ocean, then scale the foreboding cliffs to approach the desert from that direction. There were much easier options. He decided to focus on those.

The Qaenev desert was huge. Trulliç didn't know how many miles across it stood, how deep the sands ran north to south. Though Atça hadn't believed in maps, didn't trust them, he'd still shown Trulliç a recent map drawn by the emperor.

Though the emperor had much more land both to the east of the desert as well as the entire kingdom of Lydae in the north, the desert still made up a large part of the empire. Possibly as much as a quarter of the total land space, if that map was to be believed.

Though the emperor claimed the Barzhat Sea as his as well, Trulliç knew better. That belonged to the goddess Barzhat, who only sometimes suffered men to sail along the edges of the water. Trying to sail directly across was a sure way of finding the goddess's golden court, to dance before her until she gave the final kiss of release so a soul could be reborn.

Trulliç arrived in the village of Ishmirli just as twilight started. It was still spring, not full summer, so the sun set earlier than usual. Plus, he was much farther south than his home village of Gaadiwala. The sun set even earlier than he was used to.

The market stood empty, the merchants already in their homes. Trulliç didn't pass anyone on his way to the tavern. Maybe in the morning there would be more people around.

Trulliç remembered how poor Gaadiwala had seemed, particularly after he went to Çandekili, the town Yerkoyliç controlled.

Trulliç didn't want his villages to be as poor as Gaadiwala. However, there were already people living here in Ishmirli, people who had already established their routines. He didn't want to completely disrupt them by suddenly changing their wells or streets. Maybe in the morning he could bring the town together, find out what their needs were.

The tavern had a painted sign hanging in front of it—a goblet made of stone, brimming with red wine. Interesting. The Horseshoe Tavern, the tavern his family had owned, served beer primarily. Wine couldn't grow in the region, but wheat and other grains could.

Trulliç sent his senses further, beyond the village to the west. Ah. There were valleys on the very edge of the desert that would produce good grapes. Clouds and rain from the ocean would roll over the hills there, making it a green place.

Stepping inside the dim room brought many memories of his family's tavern. The rough wood tables, the clean but worn pillows scattered across the stone floor for guests, even the fireplace on the side, large enough for three men to stand in.

An older gentleman stood just beyond the stone counter that lined the back of the room. "Can I help you?" he asked. His white hair hung long around his face in the custom of the men from Lydae, though his skin was dark and his meaty hands proclaimed him as someone from the south. He wore a simple tunic made of plain brown cloth.

He paused for a moment, then took three hesitant steps forward, peering at Trulliç.

"I feel I should know you," he said softly. He blinked, then shook his head. "Sorry. Please forgive an old man whose wits are wandering. I didn't meet you, except, perhaps, in a dream."

A spike of joy pierced Trulliç. Maybe the people of the desert would know him! Everyone in Gaadiwala knew Atça.

"I am Trulliç," he said simply.

The man gasped. "The great magician!" he said, taking a step back. He gasped again. "Stay—stay right here. I'll be right back!"

The man took off through the open door.

Trulliç looked around the empty room, then down at Riyune. "So I guess I should just serve myself?"

The dog gave him an expression that could easily be read as, "Duh."

Trulliç snorted but didn't go behind the counter. He could smell the sour beer they brewed here, the remains of the flatbread they served.

What he really wanted was some good tea. Hopefully when the man got back, he'd serve Trulliç some.

After a short while the man came rushing back in the tavern. "You're still here!" he proclaimed gleefully.

Trulliç nodded. "I am." Had the man thought he'd just dreamed he'd met the great desert magician?

The tavern keeper stepped to one side and beckoned for someone else to come in.

A thin, short man entered. He had dark, thick hair that he kept oiled, in the older tradition, the ends touching the red and black *chafiyek* he wore loosely around his neck. His face had a permanent dour expression, with disapproving eyebrows and miserly lips. His dark eyes greedily sucked in Trulliç and everything he wore, discounting Riyune immediately.

"Ah, my good friend!" the man said, coming forward. "I am Gökel, the headman of this village. Welcome!"

Trulliç stood back up and bowed his head, keeping his hands at his sides. He didn't want to touch this man. He'd never really liked touching anyone.

Maybe this Gökel was a good leader, though Trulliç doubted it. He probably was the type who exaggerated the amount of tribute due to the emperor, skimming the best of it off the top and keeping it for himself.

Still, Trulliç was a stranger here. He didn't want to cause any trouble. He just wanted to meet the people of his domain. Get to know them.

And hopefully, help them.

"Brugral! Wine for our famous magician! And make it your best!" Gökel said as he came forward, ordering around the poor tavern keeper.

"Tea, please, if you have it," Trulliç insisted. He'd tasted wine—his family's tavern had served it whenever they'd acquired some barrels of it, which hadn't been too often. Sometimes, Trulliç had drank the sour beer they brewed, though he'd never developed a tasted for it.

Since arriving in the desert, he'd found what he missed most was the dark tea Atça had always served him.

Come to think of it, Yerkoyliç had also served Trulliç a delicious tea.

Was that what magicians preferred to drink?

"Have you eaten?" Gökel asked. "How can this poor host honor such an important guest?"

Trulliç blinked, surprised. Wasn't this Brugral's tavern? Or did Gökel consider the whole village his?

"Please, sit," Trulliç said, indicating one of the nearby tables, "and tell me your tales so that I might learn."

It was the traditional greeting a crowd might give a storyteller, or that a host would give a guest. However, Trulliç truly wanted to know more about Ishmirli and the people of his realm.

Brugal came over to where they sat with a platter of fresh flatbread, some finely rendered lard to spread on it, along with sliced onions and a small container of salt and spices.

"The tea will be along as soon as the water has heated," he said breathlessly. "Please, enjoy these humble refreshments in the meanwhile."

Trulliç would bet that Brugal had just served them his own dinner.

"Thank you," Trulliç said, trying to catch the man's eye to convey that he really was grateful. He wasn't sure he'd eat more than a mouthful—he didn't need to eat. But it would have been horrifically impolite of him to tell the tavern keeper that he wasn't hungry.

Gökel reached immediately for the bread and lard. Then he paused and pushed it toward Trulliç. "Here, eat," he said gruffly.

Was Gökel always the first one to eat? Trulliç had known families in Gaadiwala where that had been the case, where the head of the household ate first, then everyone else.

"Thank you," Trulliç said, amused. He would gladly break that tradition—that the highest ranked person ate first—but he also wanted to make sure that Gökel realized that Trulliç did outrank him now.

Trulliç spread the fine lard on a small piece of flatbread, added onions and a sprinkle of salt and spices. It smelled heavenly, just the faintest hint of pork remaining in the lard, the salt mixed with mint, oregano, and sage.

Brugal scurried away before Trulliç could thank him again.

Gökel watched Trulliç take his first bite before he served himself. At least he knew his manners.

"The humble village of Ishmirli is honored by your presence," Gökel told Trulliç after taking his own first bite. "How may we serve the great desert magician?"

Trulliç sighed and put the bread down. This wasn't how he wanted this meeting to go. He just wanted to come and be around people. He wasn't used to being an important person.

Suddenly, Atça taking students made more sense to Trulliç, plus why he'd agreed to teach Trulliç in the first place. Everyone else would treat Atça like an important person, not like a regular villager.

At least with his students, Atça had the opportunity to actually talk with someone as familiarity made conversations with his students less stilted.

Trulliç paused, considering. "The question is, how may I help you? The village of Ishmirli is in my territory. What do you need?"

Trulliç didn't like the greedy look that filled Gökel's eyes.

"We are a poor village," Gökel said.

Trulliç didn't snort. Gökel sounded like a storyteller in the market when he took on the wheedling tones of a shifty farmer.

"We need more money," Gökel said. "And more rain for our pastures."

"I am a desert magician," Trulliç said dryly. "I can't control the rains. Or make coins out of sand." He paused, then added, "I can build better roads so it's easier for travelers to reach Ishmirli. If there are reservoirs or aquifers under the earth, I can build more wells." He wasn't about to offer to build new houses for everyone in town, though he suspected that he could.

He also had an affinity toward glass. He could produce better lamps for the people, make them plentiful, as well as glass windows.

Gökel sniffed, as if that wasn't good enough.

Brugal appeared before their table again. While Gökel ignored the man, Trulliç asked, "Yes? What is it?"

"There's a well on the northern side of the village, next to the path to Suluvanti, that has been failing…" Brugal said hesitatingly.

"You'll have to show me in the morning," Trulliç told him, giving him an encouraging smile.

"Those people have just wasted the water there," Gökel said disparagingly.

Brugal shrugged and walked away.

"It's those people from the other side of the valley," Gökel said. "They don't belong here. Maybe you can get rid of them."

Trulliç blinked, surprised. Why would he say that? Trulliç would think that Gökel would want more people in his territory, more people that he could rule over.

Then again, he didn't know the feuds in this area. Maybe there had been fights about water rights in the past.

There was just so much to learn!

"Tell me more," Trulliç said.

No matter how Atça might have accused him of being the slowest student he had, Trulliç knew he wasn't stupid.

And though he might not know everything about Ishmirli, he could learn.

The tea Brugal brought Trulliç was truly wonderful. It smelled faintly of cinnamon and citrus, though the tea itself was black and rich. Trulliç suspected that yet again, Brugal had provided him with supplies from his own private stock, and that regular patrons of the tavern weren't served such fine tea.

In the morning, Trulliç would have to ask Brugal where bought the tea from. Trulliç would like to keep some for his tower, for the mornings when he really wanted tea.

For now, Trulliç tried to pay attention to everyone Gökel had a disagreement with. The head of the village didn't appear to like anyone. Every single person in town had slighted him at one point.

He'd seemed to assume that now that Trulliç was here, that the desert magician would get all the villagers to fall into line and do everything that Gökel demanded.

Trulliç had sat with Atça many times when he'd held court, listening to people's complaints, then casting judgments that Trulliç carefully kept in Atça's ledger books.

Did Trulliç need to set up that sort of system? A traveling court, with Trulliç going to various towns and villages and listening to their complaints?

He sighed inwardly. He supposed he should do that, though he hoped that most people could settle their own disputes.

However, he also realized that a village like Ishmirli wouldn't be able to mete out their own justice. Not with a headman like Gökel. Trulliç had developed a true antipathy for the man. How did the rest of the villagers stand him?

More importantly, why? It wasn't as if Gökel had some sort of magic and could provide the people here with a better life.

Throughout the evening, other villagers had come into the tavern for a quick drink or a word with Brugal. They'd all come to see Trulliç, he knew. However, none of them would approach the table where he sat with Gökel, afraid to intervene.

Finally, after Gökel whined about yet another slight, this time by Widow Handen, who appeared to eek out a living by tending sheep in the northern valley, Trulliç asked, exacerbated, "Who hasn't done you wrong in Ishmirli?"

Gökel sniffed. "I don't know what you mean," he said.

Trulliç shook his head. "Tell me about the good people here," he said plainly.

Gökel shrugged. "Everyone has their good and bad points," he said.

"True," Trulliç admitted. "But you can still tell me something good," he insisted. "Tell me something that has delighted you in the last few days."

"Life isn't always fun and games," Gökel growled. "There's hard work to be done. A man's duty."

Trulliç looked at the man sitting next to him. Trulliç knew he looked just a boy in comparison—after all, he'd just turned eighteen.

He wasn't completely naïve, however.

And Gökel seemed to have forgotten his place, had stopped acting like a generous host at some point during the evening. He'd begun to believe that this was still his village, not Trulliç's.

Trulliç bent down, glancing over at Riyune who sat perfectly still, like a statue, next to him.

The dog was no help, as usual.

Then Trulliç scooped up a bit of sand from the floor and spilled it onto the table.

Gökel didn't seem to notice, was still ranting about how no one appreciated him. Including Trulliç, evidently.

Trulliç had had enough.

The edges of the wood table had been slicked over, softened by many hands and bellies rubbing against it over the years. The center of the flat surface felt more rough. Trulliç carefully slid his finger across it, through the small pile of sand. The table probably wasn't rough enough that he'd get a splinter. Probably.

"Enough," Trulliç said, interrupting Gökel.

"What do you—" the man sputtered.

"I said enough," Trulliç growled as he drew a circle in the sand with his finger. "I'm not here to punish people at your whim."

"Then what are you here for, boy?" Gökel sneered. "What can you do for the fine people of Ishmirli? If you can't make it rain and you can't give us more coin?"

Riyune suddenly pushed his head against Trulliç's knee. Words didn't come through clearly, not like on the other two times when the dog had spoken to Trulliç.

The feeling was still there. The urging for Trulliç to just do it. Riyune would be there, would support him.

The words fell from Trulliç's lips before he could stop them. "I could get rid of you," he said softly. "I think the fine people of Ishmirli might thank me for that."

The sand he'd drawn up onto the table sprang up into a mini-whirlwind, not much taller than the span of Trulliç's palm.

"Oh, really?" Gökel said. He didn't seem frightened of the magic Trulliç was performing. Maybe he'd been expecting something more grand. "And what? Replace me with old Brugal, there?" Gökel laughed, a high, nasty sound.

"Yes," Trulliç said simply.

"I dare you," Gökel said.

When Trulliç didn't reply, Gökel snorted in derision. "I didn't think you had it in you. You're just a boy, trying to fill a man's role."

Trulliç nodded. "You're half right. I am still learning how to be a man. But I know my role."

He was the desert magician. He needed to take care of his people.

The fine people of Ishmirli needed a much, much better headman.

He could help with that.

Trulliç cupped his hand around the mini-whirlwind and casually threw it at the man sitting next to him.

Gökel started choking.

It was so easy—far too easy—for the rage inside of Trulliç to leap up and join the sand already choking the man. For Trulliç's anger to add winds that pushed the sand deeper down the man's throat.

After a few long moments, Gökel stopped choking and fell to the side. Trulliç called up more winds to pick up the body and carried it far out into the desert, where it would feed the creatures there, the hawks and mice, the snakes and lizards.

Brugal stood shocked, as still as a mouse before a desert hawk.

"And what will you do with me?" he asked, his voice breaking.

"Do you want to be the village headman?" Trulliç asked in return.

Brugal gave an obvious gulp. Then his eyes grew more shrewd. "Maybe."

He nodded his head toward the open door.

Trulliç realized belatedly that other villagers had been standing there. Watching. Judging.

"You've scared them but good," Brugal told him. "And you still scare me."

"That wasn't what I meant to do!" Trulliç said, horrified. What had he done?

Brugal was right, though. One of Trulliç's first acts as the desert magician had been to kill someone.

That wasn't what he'd intended to do, not at all. He didn't want his people to be afraid of him, tiptoeing around him, scared that they would be the next to die.

"I've been listening to you all night. I think you have a good heart." Brugal paused, then added, "And that we can work together."

Trulliç nodded slowly. "How can I make it up to them?" Was it possible to show them that he wasn't a scary, vengeful magician?

Brugal finally smiled at him, his first true smile of the evening. "Honestly? Between you and me? You already made a good start by getting rid of that braggart. He was the headman here because his father had, and his grandfather before that. His son would have tried to assume the same role, though I don't think people here would have stood for it." Brugal put his hands on his hips and regarded Trulliç. "However, you've also done great damage by listening to him first. We'll have to fix that in the morning."

Trulliç nodded. He'd be happy to work with Brugal on that.

To fix this mess he'd just made.

CHAPTER FOUR

NADEEM

NADEEM HAPPILY RODE WITH THE caravan for a week. But now it was time for her to continue her journey on her own. She checked the bags strapped to Banut, her sweet female camel, making sure they were tight but not too tight. Darkness had just kissed the sky, hiding the clear blue with night. Only a few stars twinkled on the horizon. The air felt softer here, along the oasis trail, since they no longer traveled across hot sands.

She wore the traveling clothes she'd picked up at the first town the caravan had visited. She was dressed like a merchant, actually—with loose black pants and a short, navy-blue tunic over a light-weight, white blouse. Her *chafiyek* lay around her neck, a finely woven cloth with blue, black, and white squares. Tough leather sandals with thick soles that she could easily run in covered her feet. A heavy cloak was tied to Banut's back for when the night grew chilly. Along with what appeared to be a stout walking stick, though Nadeem could still see the snake-headed cane at the heart of the illusion.

"Must you go?" came a quiet voice to her left.

Nadeem didn't startle, though she hadn't known anyone was there.

However, she'd been expecting Levent's visit.

"I must," she said simply as she buckled the pack on Banut's right side. "There are things I must do."

Namely, go and visit Aunt Parayat in Kardeş, the hidden oasis of the star sisters. To find out if there was already a price on her head for turning her back on the rest of her sisters. For not fulfilling her oath to Atça.

To see if she could get her wily aunt to answer some of Nadeem's burning questions.

Levent came closer, standing beside her. He put a reassuring hand on Banut's flank. The merchant had a way with animals. Though Banut hadn't been nervous, she shifted her stance so her legs were wider and she appeared to relax further.

He wore his usual merchant's outfit, a tunic slit down the center in the southern style made out of dark green, over brown loose trousers and solid sandals. His black hair curled slightly around his face, giving him a younger smile.

"When will I see you again?" he asked plainly, though his tone held a caressing note.

"When the gods will it," Nadeem replied, giving him the usual response that storytellers did in their tales when lovers parted. He'd been her first male lover. Gentle and different than the women she'd known. She hadn't decided yet which she liked better, male or female, or if she'd ever choose. Both had their advantages.

Levent's smile broadened. "I shall count the days," he said, continuing the litany. Then he grew more serious. "I am on my way to Hayalevi, to see the great towers of the desert magician."

"Trulliç," Nadeem told him. "I will go there too, someday."

When she could face her failure. When even his name didn't put her ill at ease.

Levent tilted his head to the side. "You know him?" His eyes narrowed.

Oh goddess, he wasn't jealous, was he? They'd made no promises to one another, no vows or bonds. Nadeem had been warned that men would be like this.

"Of course I know Trulliç," Nadeem said, putting as much disdain into her voice as she could. "He's the magician of all of Qaenev," Implying that all desert people would know him.

Levent nodded slowly. "But you aren't a star sister anymore," he said.

Nadeem shrugged. "I grew up in an oasis." She was still of the desert, would always think of herself that way. More so now that she'd rubbed enchanted sand into her mangled cheek.

The wound still hurt now and again, a brilliant flare of pain that always caught her off guard. If she wasn't careful, she'd gasp when it struck instead of maintaining a stoic mien.

The pain had grown less and her skin had started healing.

Her affinity toward the desert had grown greater.

Trulliç could accurately point in the direction of the closest water, no matter where he stood on the sands. Nadeem had begun to acquire that ability. If water ran miles and miles away, she might not be able to smell it on the air.

If it was closer, though, she could walk in a straight line to it.

She knew that other desert creatures had the same ability, to always be able to sense water. Humans were the only ones not gifted that way. They needed to learn where the oasis rivers ran.

Nadeem knew where they lay now, without a map.

Levent smiled at her and shook his head. "No, you knew Trulliç from some other time. Before he became the desert magician." He paused, then sighed. "I hope that you will tell me, someday."

Nadeem shrugged again. Her past was her own. Levent had hinted before that he'd like to know what had happened to her, why she'd turned her back on the star sisters and labeled herself merely a traveler, now.

While Nadeem was happy to share her bed with him, she didn't feel the need to do more than that.

"Be on your way, then, mysterious stranger," Levent said as he bowed his head and stepped back. "May our paths cross again before the next rains."

Nadeem looked over her shoulder at him. "I do thank you for your most excellent hospitality," she said seriously.

"It was my pleasure," Levent said, giving her a sweep bow this time. "And I hope to see you in the spring in Hayalevi. Even if at that point I'll just be a plain merchant while you'll still be a mysterious stranger on even more mysterious business, dealing with the desert magician and no one else."

Nadeem couldn't help her shiver. Levent may be right. Once she finished with her individual business with Aunt Parayat, she might have to go to Hayalevi.

To warn Trulliç that he, too, had even more of a price on his head.

Nadeem swung her foot up into the mounting stirrup, then pulled herself over Banut's back. Most needed mounting blocks, but Nadeem had trained herself to do without.

"Safe journeys and easy water," Levent called up to her.

"Good trade and easy water for you, too," Nadeem replied.

She paused for a moment, then shrugged. What did it matter if Levent saw her do magic? He would keep her secrets, she knew. Even if he told anyone, who would believe a merchant's wild tales?

Nadeem lifted her hands up in front of her and *blurred* her fingers, making the outline of her skin indistinct. Then she lowered her hands to either side of Banut's neck and did the same thing.

She heard Levent's gasp, but she wasn't done yet.

She added shadows to them both. Darkening them. Hiding them. Making them part of the night.

Levent stood perfectly still, aware that he'd witnessed a rare display. No star sister would ever have changed like that in front of a stranger.

And anyone who was not of the *kabil* was considered a stranger. No matter how familiar they might be.

Then Levent gave her a third bow, low and held deeply for a moment. "Until I see you again. At your wish, obviously."

Levent turned and walked back toward the camp, still shaking his head.

Nadeem smiled. It had been a pleasant interlude to ride with the caravan at dawn and dusk, to lay with Levent during the heat of the day, to not worry about destinies and blood oaths for a while.

It was time for her to get going though, back to her life.

To gather up the remains of it, see what she had left, and travel forward again.

Nadeem waited in the shade of a boulder, Banut seated beside her, watching Kardeş. Or rather, watching the guards. She was familiar with the pattern they ran: two obvious watchers who let themselves be seen now and again, with a third secreted away that none could see.

Someone patient enough to wait through two changes of guards would eventually note the third.

Or perhaps not. She was well hidden and never joined the other two, even when she was relieved of her duty.

Few had that patience, however. Fewer still would have found Kardeş in the first place.

A caravan following the oasis trail that stretched north and south of Kardeş would pass far to the east, not noticing where the water split. Even if they managed to stumble upon the second stream, the star sisters kept the oasis itself hidden. Even to Nadeem's eye, the bushes that marked the edge of the oasis all shimmered, giving the appearance of a mirage. If the guards spotted anyone coming, the entire village would simply vanish.

Nadeem waited until the end of the next shift of guards, just as dusk approached, when the watchers would be tired and bored, not guarding as carefully, before she made her move.

She'd already strengthened her own illusion, blurring her edges and hiding her face in shadows. She cast further illusions on Banut, keeping her hidden by the rocks. The camel wouldn't move but would stay where she was, at least for a few hours.

Nadeem tied the snake-headed walking stick to her back. Carrying it was the surest way of hiding her steps from Trulliç. She had no idea if it would help or hinder with the star sisters. She suspected neither—they weren't of the desert, no matter what she'd told Levent.

Not like she was.

Taking a deep breath, Nadeem pushed herself up to her toes a few times, stretching out her calves. Anxious anticipation settled deep in her belly.

Could she slip into the oasis undetected? The star sisters' home? The most heavily defended place in the entire empire, save that of the emperor's palace itself?

Only one way to find out…

Nadeem took a few more moments to stretch, then started her race across the open sands, going as fast as she could, her heart singing with the joy of the wind.

Nadeem could admit to herself that she was disappointed when nothing happened when she stepped into Kardeş. The oasis wasn't separate from the desert.

She realized that she'd been hoping that there would be as distinct a border between the oasis and the desert. That the star sisters' home was somehow different from the other villages and towns in Trulliç's domain.

It wasn't, however.

Trulliç could still find them, appear in the middle of their tents. And they wouldn't be able to turn him away.

Nadeem crouched down next to a large cactus and paused. No alarm sounded. No one had seen her. She took a deep breath of relief. The smell of the village filled her, the sweet scents of the cooking fires and the sweat of girls, spices, and sheep.

Now, where would she find Aunt Parayat? Dusk was fast approaching. Hopefully she'd be in her tent, where she'd napped through the heat of the afternoon.

If she was still alive. That had always been Nadeem's fear, that at some point her aunt wouldn't awaken from one of her naps.

Nadeem rushed there as fast as she could. Nothing had changed, at least not in the three plus years she'd been at the training camp on Knife Ridge. The cooking tents still sat to the east where the tallest trees stood, the area in the oasis that would cool the soonest in the afternoon. Next to them lay a wide open area with many long tables and benches, where the sisters would gather together and eat.

The teaching tents lay to the north of there, and the private tents of the teachers lay to the south.

While the younger sisters stayed mostly in communal tents, the aunts generally had private ones. Some still chose to live together, old friends who couldn't bear to be separated, in groups of three or four.

Aunt Parayat had always lived apart, at least as long as Nadeem had known her.

Nadeem had to pause while a group of laughing aunts walked past her, heading toward the cooking tents. They walked arm in arm, comrades.

A pang of jealousy went through Nadeem. She would never enjoy such sisterhood, not ever again.

Then she steeled herself. It was better this way.

The tent flap for Aunt Parayat's tent stood open. There was something off about it. But what?

Ah. That was it. There was an illusion cast around the opening. Most would see the tent flap as closed.

Wait.

Before, it had been so easy for Nadeem to cast illusions of grand warriors and throw herself into battle. The small, mundane things had always been so difficult.

Had her aunt grown so much weaker that Nadeem had to look twice in order to even detect the illusion?

Or had Nadeem grown impossibly strong?

She suspected the latter, but she didn't have time to make certain.

With one more deep breath, Nadeem slipped inside the tent.

It looked the same as it always had: a small square, about twelve feet on a side, with a few personal possessions. The brown tent fabric had always made the space feel cooler than the outside. The sand floor had two thick, large rugs on it, beaten clean regularly so the black-and-blue braid was visible. A distaff full of fiber, ready for spinning, stood next to a pile of baskets containing small balls of yarn.

At the back, Aunt Parayat had a fluffed mattress full of down feathers that she slept on. She'd woven her blankets herself, so they had unusual geometric patterns and odd colors as she'd experimented through the years.

Nadeem smelled the lanolin of the wool and realized that scent, as much as anything else, told her that she was home.

Her aunt lay on her mattress, still napping, her torso naked while her hips and legs were covered with a thin sheet. Many more lines crossed her face than the last time Nadeem had seen her. Her soft pink mouth was open, making her look unbelievably vulnerable. White curls surrounded her head. Her arms still had muscles, but the tanned skin sagged with age.

Before Nadeem could reach out and touch her aunt, make sure she was still alive, Aunt Parayat opened her eyes. The faded brown stared directed into Nadeem's.

"Hello, Nadeem," Aunt Parayat said very quietly. "I've been expecting you."

Nadeem withdrew to the far side of Aunt Parayat's tent while her aunt sat up, stretched, and slipped on a light-weight tunic to cover her nakedness. The tunic had been woven recently from unbleached thread, with hints of black, brown, gold, and green running through it, specks of color that hadn't coalesced into a pattern.

Would the weavers change their patterns now that Trulliç had found his home? His colors would be gold and green, that much Nadeem knew.

Aunt Parayat walked up to Nadeem, holding out her hands in greeting. "It's good to see you," she assured the younger woman.

They grasped arms like comrades at war, clasping each other's forearms tightly. Nadeem felt assured that her aunt's arms still felt like steel despite how soft her skin had gotten.

But her aunt had also shrunk in the past three years. Nadeem had never been taller than Aunt Parayat before this.

"It is good to see you as well," Nadeem told her former mentor.

"I have little to offer you here," Aunt Parayat said, indicating the tent. "Beyond fresh water and hungry ears."

Nadeem smiled. It was one of the calls a crowd made to a storyteller, offering to quench his or her thirst while they dealt with a different sort of need.

"I'm not sure you'll be happy to hear what I have to say," Nadeem said. She raised her head then turned it slowly, so Aunt Parayat could see her mangled cheek. "I am merely a traveler, now."

The words hurt. Much more than Nadeem had ever imagined they would.

Aunt Parayat still held onto Nadeem's arms fiercely. "There are worse things," she said darkly. "Much, much worse."

Nadeem's relief made her knees buckle.

"Though you are no longer of the *kabil*," Aunt Parayat said as she led Nadeem to the side, indicating that she should sit in the place of honor, "I still declare you friend."

"Thank you," Nadeem whispered, her sudden tears choking her words. "I am honored by your friendship."

"Sit," Aunt Parayat said.

When Nadeem would have protested, Aunt Parayat pointed to the pillows. "Guests of honor sit there. And they show respect to their elders by following their requests. Particularly old women who have little patience."

"Yes, ma'am," Nadeem said as meekly as she could, sitting quickly.

"We don't have much time, I'm afraid," Aunt Parayat admitted as she sat beside her former student. "While I will engage with you, many would declare you a traitor."

Nadeem nodded. Aunt Izmet, the one who'd trained Nadeem to be one of the emperor's stars, would have killed her rather than talk with her.

But Aunt Izmet believed in following all orders fanatically, rather than questioning.

"Did you dream of me coming to see you?" Nadeem asked. If her arrival had prompted her aunt to dream of her, others may have shared the same dream.

Aunt Parayat shook her head. "No. I just know you well enough. You would return when Aunt Izmet's teaching and training failed you."

"Why did you send me off with her?" Nadeem asked, though her aunt hadn't pushed her that direction. Not really.

Aunt Parayat's quiet laughter filled the tent. "As if I could have stopped you," she said. "No, you were destined to become one of the emperor's stars from the moment you took over Aunt Haneet's lesson, showing such strong magical ability when you were so young." She paused, then added, "It was why I took on your lessons personally. So that you might have a chance against the brainwashing Aunt Izmet would try to give you."

"The questions," Nadeem stated. "Always asking questions." Her aunt had never let anything be. She'd always had questions, and then more questions, for Nadeem, forcing her to think beyond what she'd been told.

"Exactly," Aunt Parayat said. "It was my fervent hope that encouraging your questioning nature would inoculate you."

"Against what?" Nadeem asked. There had to be more to her aunt's schemes. There always was. Plans within plans.

Aunt Parayat reached up, moving so slowly Nadeem didn't flinch when her aunt touched her chin and gently turned her face so that she could see the mangled mark there. "It glistens, you know," Aunt Parayat said quietly before she dropped her hand. "A faint glow of magic. Like a male magician might have."

Nadeem stiffened. She knew she'd grown powerful, that her magic possibly had expanded beyond mere illusions.

Normally, a star sister would be killed if they'd grown that strong. It wasn't natural.

She grimaced. She'd become an abomination.

"Stop that," Aunt Parayat said, pinching the flesh on Nadeem's arm hard enough to make her wince. "You aren't a pariah. You are something different."

Nadeem waited, willing her aunt to give her a clue as to what she should become. What trails were open to her now.

Aunt Parayat dropped her gaze to her own hands, grasped tightly in front of her. "The emperor," she said after another long moment, "is evil."

Nadeem blinked, more startled than if her aunt had suddenly declared herself pregnant.

"Why would you say that?" Nadeem asked finally into the chilled silence.

"I've met him," Aunt Parayat said, turning her gaze from her hands to Nadeem. Her eyes burned with a fever Nadeem had never seen before. "He thinks he's a god, or can become one. He will destroy not just the Tanesh empire, but the entire world. You must stop him."

"How?" Nadeem asked. "I can't attack him. He has my blood." Like all babies born with power, a blood hound had followed her mother around and gobbled up the afterbirth, carrying it to the emperor for him to fashion a scale from.

Aunt Parayat's eyes narrowed. "Your blood is not the same as it once was," she said simply.

Nadeem didn't know how to respond to that. Her aunt was correct.

But how could she challenge the *Padisha-i-Ghazi*? The great emperor himself?

"You stay here and rest," Aunt Parayat said, rising. "I will bring you food for your continued journeys."

Nadeem swallowed hard. She would admit that a part of her had hoped that she'd be welcomed here in Kardeş, and that she'd find a place among her sisters.

She should have known that her mentor would have other plans for her. A destiny to fulfill. Yet another blood oath, though one that shook her to her core.

Some part of her nearly giggled as part of an old call-and-response song drifted through her head, of how a woman's work was never done.

And neither was hers.

Nadeem slept fitfully on Aunt Parayat's down-filled mattress, her dreams filled with visions of the end of the world, as always.

Only this time, she fought not only the darkness but the star sisters as well.

The emperor had infected her former sisters with his darkness. They danced to their deaths under her blade, laughing and unconcerned about the sweet kiss of night. Their sweat and blood covered Nadeem. Each drop that touched her cheek weakened her, draining away her magic, until nothing remained except her will.

She became her sword at that point, the steel directing her, dancing on its own, until the goddess Barzhat picked her up and wielded her.

But eventually, even the goddess stumbled during the onslaught.

There were just too many of the sisters, with an endless army marching over the sands.

After she died, Nadeem's soul flew over the sands to the edges of the star sister army. She saw in horror that the aunts marked the cheeks of all who came to them with brands of fire—old and young, men and women alike. The first touch changed them into girls, star sisters given knowledge and power without earning it.

The abomination woke Nadeem. She sat up, still shivering.

The tent had grown dark, the night pressing in on all sides. A simple clay lamp illuminated the room. Aunt Parayat sat patiently beside the mattress where Nadeem lay.

"You went deep," Aunt Parayat told Nadeem as she handed her a water skin.

Nadeem merely nodded, ashamed. She'd always been reluctant to share her visions, humiliated that they controlled her instead of the other way around.

Since she'd rubbed the desert sands into her cheek, they'd grown worse. Deeper. Longer. And always about the death of the world.

"I couldn't walk beside you," Aunt Parayat told her. "Tell me what you saw, so that I might learn."

Nadeem took another drink of water instead of immediately answering her aunt. What could she say?

"Please," Aunt Parayat said as she settled herself into a cross-legged pose. "Share what you have seen."

"The end of the world," Nadeem whispered, afraid to speak the words out loud. "Always. The end of the world. Gibbering darkness set loose by the emperor. Corrupting people. The star sisters. Even the gods."

Aunt Parayat nodded. "The emperor seeks the desert heart," she said. "The heart that tamed the darkness."

"That was what Trulliç said," Nadeem replied, not surprised that her aunt knew.

Aunt Parayat tilted her head to one side. "Trulliç," she breathed out. "Ah. That explains much of your change."

Nadeem waited while Aunt Parayat considered her anew. When it seemed that her mentor wouldn't say anything more, Nadeem added, "Atça, Trulliç's mentor, hired me to kill Trulliç if it turned out that the boy was disloyal to the emperor."

Aunt Parayat shrugged. "That is your business, and yours alone. Both the judgment and the deed. As you are no longer a star sister, it is not possible for you to fulfill a blood oath."

Nadeem stiffened. "Atça may call for another to fulfill it, then."

"That would be his right," Aunt Parayat said. "Would you fight the next star sister who came to kill Trulliç?"

"I wouldn't have to," Nadeem said with a tight smile. "She wouldn't get ten feet into the desert without Trulliç knowing. And he could defend himself."

"Is he that powerful?" Aunt Parayat asked, curious.

"Not yet. But he will be," Nadeem assured her. Even if she wasn't there to knock some sense into him, maybe that dog of his would.

Nadeem reached just past the sleeping mat and picked up the snake-headed walking stick. She cut the illusion to it and handed it to her aunt.

Aunt Parayat gasped when she grasped it. "Why do you carry this cursed thing?"

"It was a gift from the emperor, given to the man I'd been assigned to kill, as part of my first mission," Nadeem told her. It pleased her that she wasn't the only one who didn't trust the magic embodied by the cane.

"Did you kill him?" Aunt Parayat asked.

Nadeem wasn't sure about the casual tone in her aunt's voice. Obviously the question held much more importance than her aunt wanted to let on.

"I did not. I failed," Nadeem replied, her words still tasting bitter. "My team had to do it instead."

Aunt Parayat leaned forward and squeezed Nadeem's arm. "Good," she said. "I have too many souls weighing me down when I reach the goddess's golden court. It is better for you not to have any."

Nadeem nodded. Aunt Izmet would have told her that since the emperor had ordered the killing, the weight of the soul would be balanced against the emperor's wishes. That she wouldn't have been burdened with it after she died.

There were many things that Aunt Izmet said that Nadeem no longer believed.

"Still, why do you carry this, then?" Aunt Parayat said, handing the walking stick back to Nadeem. "It feels cursed, like it carries dark deeds in its heart."

It always amazed Nadeem how slippery the wood felt, as if it wasn't really of this world. "It hides my steps from Trulliç," she said. She wasn't sure why Aunt Parayat said it was cursed—that wasn't the feeling she got from it at all.

"You need to show him this," Aunt Parayat told her firmly. "He needs to know that the emperor can hide himself from the desert magician. Could possibly disguise an entire army marching across the sands."

Nadeem gasped. She hadn't considered that aspect of the walking stick or thought about more than just her need.

She shook her head. All her training was failing her. Her teachings that always made her consider the entire *kabil* and not just herself.

"So are you just going to sit there and feel sorry for yourself?" Aunt Parayat's voice came through Nadeem's haze with the sting of a whip.

"I don't want to kill the emperor," Nadeem whispered, speaking her heart's ache.

"Then don't," Aunt Parayat said with a shrug. "You merely have to stop him from acquiring the desert heart. From loosening that gibbering darkness on the world that you've always had visions of."

Nadeem swallowed against a suddenly dry throat.

Her aunt was correct. Nadeem didn't have to actually kill the emperor. All she had to do was to stop him. Somehow.

"You don't have to do it by yourself," Aunt Parayat said gently. "You have friends who can help. Like Trulliç."

Nadeem shook her head. None in her team would help—they'd all fallen into Aunt Izmet's trap, would only listen to her. They would consider Nadeem a traitor. None here in Kadeş would call her friend either, besides Aunt Parayat.

Was Trulliç a friend? She'd been hired to kill him, after all.

Maybe he wouldn't hold that against her. She had told him of his true home.

"I will stop the emperor," Nadeem said, aware that her words, no matter how quietly spoken, rang like a blood oath through the empty space of the tent. "He shall not have the desert heart."

Aunt Parayat gave her a proud smile, the same a mother would give a daughter after the birth of her first son.

Though Nadeem had no idea how she would fulfill her oath, she knew it was the most important one she'd ever taken. Even if it involved no blood.

CHAPTER FIVE

TRULLIÇ

TRULLIÇ SLEPT FITFULLY UNDER THE stars outside the tavern, next to the cold kitchen ovens. Brugal had offered Trulliç his own room in the tavern. However, Trulliç couldn't sleep in a room. He suspected that he'd never be able to sleep inside ever again. He needed to be able to see the stars. More now than ever before.

The strange smells of burnt bread and the sounds of people around him kept him awake. He almost left more than once, wanting to step outside of the village just so he could breathe again.

But he'd already done so much damage by killing Gökel. The people were afraid of him. What would they do if he didn't spend the night but disappeared and reappeared? Would more stories of him grow, stories of him going off and killing other village headmen?

Hopefully his people wouldn't always be afraid of him. He wanted for people to treat him like how the people in Çandekili had treated their wizard, with respect but also with great fondness.

If only Atça had let Trulliç come into his power sooner! Maybe Trulliç wouldn't have started out his rule on such bad footing.

Before the dawn filled the sky, Trulliç went to sit on the front stoop of the tavern. Brugal came downstairs shortly afterward. He seemed surprised that Trulliç had already risen.

"What can this humble host offer such an esteemed guest?" Brugal asked.

"Merely some more of that excellent tea," Trulliç replied. "And tell me where you got it, so that I might purchase more." Trulliç didn't have much money on him. He hoped that the people in the market would barter for glass lamps or windows instead.

"I will take you to the stall this afternoon," Brugal promised. "This morning, however, if we could go north of town to look at that well?"

"Of course!" Trulliç said, grateful that he might be able to make up for his early impression.

After Brugal brought the black spiced tea, they stayed seated on the front step. Brugal greeted everyone who walked up by name and introduced them Trulliç. It felt casual and friendly, much more how Trulliç had wanted to meet people. Riyune stayed seated beside him, acting like a normal dog, reaching out his head to sniff offered fingers, scratching himself, even yawning and rolling in the dirt from time to time.

Brugal told the people who came by that he and Trulliç would be heading up toward the northern-most well in a little while, and that they'd be in the market that afternoon. Many rushed off at the news.

Trulliç hoped there would be easy water near the well. That he'd be able to show the village that he could do something positive for them.

And not just kill.

***

Though the village of Ishmirli was richer than Gaadiwala, it was still a small, poor village. Gökel hadn't been lying about that. The huts had more wood than the ones in Trulliç's hometown. The people used it for making fences, tables, and benches. Trees were more readily available from just over the hills. Plus, cottonwood grew near the stream that ran east of Ishmirli.

The streets were all dirt and sand, not gravel. Spring grass covered the nearby hills, bright green but already browning. Scrawny chickens scattered in front of them or called from their yards. No other dogs dared approach Riyune, but even from a distance Trulliç could count the ribs in their skinny sides. Goats and sheep bleated from nearby pastures, tough scavengers looking for their next meal.

Trulliç tried to get a sense of how the houses were laid out. In Gaadiwala, they were all clustered around the wells. In Ishmirli that seemed to be part of it, but the neighborhoods also seemed to be dictated by families: first one small hut added onto a larger house, then another, and another, until it became a sprawling compound.

A crowd of people followed Trulliç and Brugal as they walked north along the main street. This was the path traders would take, going from the port to the south to the larger towns and villages to the north. Trulliç cleared the path of sharp stones as he walked, pushing them unobtrusively into the dirt. Not just so it would be easier for him to walk, but so that all who walked would find the path clear.

He wasn't sure if anyone noticed. He wasn't about to call attention to it, however. Let the people discover it later, marvel at his passing. It was the least he could do.

The well stood at the top of a small rise. Huts clustered to both the right and left of it, beyond the road. Trulliç recognized that the people in this neighborhood weren't as well off as those closer to the center of the village. They hung plain bolts of cloth over their doors instead of proper wood. The stone walls needed attention, the spring rains melting the mortar. No chickens squawked at them, and the children all ran away as they approached.

The well itself had originally been built out of fine brick that had cracked with age. A stone trellis had been built above the well with a rusted winch for lowering and raising water buckets.

Past the collection of huts the track ran straight and true. Trulliç turned and looked back over Ishmirli. He'd have to visit Gökel's compound later—he assumed that was the larger set of houses off to the east. The market could be seen as well, an open area surrounded by a cluster of buildings. The other taller buildings probably held temples that he should also visit.

"This is the well?" Trulliç asked Brugal in a loud voice so everyone who had followed them up the hill could hear.

"It is. Can you fix it, magician?" Brugal asked in return.

"I will try," Trulliç promised the man.

He beckoned for Riyune to come closer.

People who hadn't seen the dog before or realized that Trulliç traveled with a companion, gasped as Riyune came walking up.

Riyune gave the equivalent of a doggie eye roll, then he sat beside Trulliç and did his statue imitation. It didn't bother Trulliç when Riyune froze that way, though he was aware that it unnerved some people.

Trulliç tentatively reached out his hand and touched his fingertips to the top of Riyune's head, feeling Riyune's warm, smooth fur.

All the land came more alive. Trulliç felt more connected to it, the sand and the dirt, the scrubby trees and the small life. He wasn't as aware of the people in front of him—just had tenuous ties to them. Would those grow stronger? He hoped so.

Why did that always happen whenever Trulliç touched Riyune's fur? Why did the desert dog create such a strong connection for him?

He would have to try to figure that out at some other point.

For now, he had a job to do.

Trusting that Riyune would keep him anchored above ground, Trulliç pushed his senses under the ground, diving down the shaft of the well and into the water below.

It was obvious to him that the water levels had dropped and the reservoir had started to dry up. Why?

Trulliç easily navigated the branching stream that fed the water table. No other source pulled at the water, not that he could find. The reservoir was just old and tired. Not enough spring rains had fallen to refill it, not just for this past year but for several seasons. No new streams had formed to fill it.

Disappointment washed over Trulliç. He nearly gave up at that point. He couldn't cause the rains to fall, to bring water where there wasn't any. However, he didn't want to disappoint the village. Particularly not after he'd made such a blunder the night before.

He caused his awareness to flow back to where he'd started, just under the well. Instead of following the obvious path, he pushed deeper into the earth. Maybe under the original reservoir would be a secondary source, another spring.

Riyune leaned against Trulliç's leg, up where his body still stood.

Was Riyune following along? How did the dog do that?

It took Trulliç a moment to figure out what the dog had seen.

There. Not directly under the well, but to the south. A large untapped reservoir. And it was already part of the village. He wouldn't be taking another man's water.

It didn't take much power to push aside the strong boulders and hard-packed clay, then to cause the body of water to flow his direction.

Trulliç heard the water bubbling in the well even as he drew his awareness back into his body.

"There's water again!" Brugal proudly announced.

The people gave a ragged cheer. Trulliç wondered why it wavered so. Was it because they were afraid of him?

He peered at the gathered crowd curiously. They didn't seem afraid of him. Rather, they seemed shocked. Had they not believed that he could do such a thing?

But they knew him. He was the desert magician. They were his people.

A young woman broke free of the crowd and came forward. She wore a clean but faded tunic of dull blue over a full black skirt, her *chafiyek* the only piece of clothing somewhat new and a pretty green. She had the long hair of a married woman, braided over her shoulder, with an infant tied to her back.

"May I?" she asked, hefting her water jug and pointing with her chin toward the well.

"Please," Trulliç said, stepping to the side.

She lowered the old bucket, splashing it into the water, then drawing it out. She then cupped her hands and offered Trulliç the first drink from the well.

Trulliç wasn't sure why this felt like such an important ritual. But he lowered his head and drank from her palms.

The water was just water. Plain, cool, refreshing. It wasn't like the water from the cavern that had cleared away all his bad dreams, opened up the desert to him.

Still, it made Trulliç laugh delightedly, particularly after the woman then lifted her hands and drank as well.

The woman blushed and bowed her head. "Thank you, Trulliç," she said softly. "We needed the water."

Trulliç turned back to the well. He rebuilt the bricks, hardened the stone trellis. The well would stand for a long time, now.

"Are there other wells that need repair?" Trulliç called out.

"Gökel's sure doesn't," a man said. The people around him laughed rudely.

Trulliç nodded. Gökel had probably only kept his own well in good repair. "I'll visit them all," Trulliç promised.

That brought a stronger cheer.

Trulliç looked over at Brugal, who shrugged. "We'll do that next," he said.

A parade formed, in front and behind them, as they made their way from one well to the next. Not all the wells needed more water or better access to the reservoirs beneath them. They did all need some repairs that Trulliç gladly did, strengthening walls and bricks, trellis and buckets.

No one offered him water again. It made him strangely sad that no one else claimed such familiarity with him and instead held him at arm's distance.

That was all right. The people here would get to know him. They would grow more comfortable with him and would come to understand that he wasn't always to be feared.

<hr>

As the afternoon drew long shadows from the buildings, Trulliç led Brugal and the villagers who still followed them to the edge of Ishmirli where the foothills faced the desert to the east. Trulliç breathed in the open air, the scents of the sand, his chest loosening for the first time in a day.

"Stay here," Trulliç told Brugal as he walked a few steps away, drawing closer to the desert. He turned to face the villagers.

Then he unstrapped the glass horseshoe that he wore tied to his belt.

He realized that he didn't need to tie it to himself anymore. The glass horseshoe was part of him, now. It would follow after him, bobbing along in the air like a small dog if he ever dropped it.

It was good to know that he couldn't lose it out here in the desert. It was too important, too much a part of him, though it still had very little magic in itself.

He held up the horseshoe, drawing everyone's attention to it. "Mothers use horseshoes to draw out their babes," he said loudly, aware of the legend he built. "My mother had planned on me to stay in the north, where my father was from. She bought a horseshoe made of tin from one of the local mines."

The people stirred, their feet shuffling, almost as one. Even in the dimming light they knew what he carried wasn't tin.

"The blood hound who attended her transformed the horseshoe from tin to glass," Trulliç said.

The crowd gasped quietly.

"Let me share my gift with you, now," Trulliç said. While the water and the wells had been good, important, the people needed to have his token as well. Just as the people in Yerkoyliç's city had emblems of flowers, birds, and bees, his people needed to understand glass.

Trulliç turned his back on the villagers and raised both of his hand over his head. The horseshoe tugged at his finger. He released it, allowing it to float above his head.

Great sheets of sand built in front of Trulliç, wave upon wave of them. He blasted them with heat and magic, forcing them to collapse down on themselves, forming hundreds of glass balls. Ones that fit in his palm and clear with just a single ribbon of gold or green. Solid black marbles not much bigger than the tip of his pinky. Large balls bigger than his head and striped in different colors.

The balls bobbed in the air, then started to disperse. Most flew toward the villagers. Trulliç heard people laugh with delight as they snagged their own glass ball from the air.

Some of the balls burrowed under the sand. Trulliç understood that they would stand guard on the borders of Qaenev, challenge those who would challenge him.

The rest flew past the villagers in attendance. Trulliç knew they'd find their way into the homes of the people of Ishmirli who weren't attending him.

Everyone would have glass in their homes. Not just the balls, but lamps and windows as well. Trulliç would make sure of it.

He felt the villagers more solidly, as if they'd suddenly become part of the land. His heart swelled with joy as they cheered.

He was truly the desert magician, now.

It didn't surprise Trulliç that the woman who'd offered him water from the first well appeared outside the tavern the next morning before the sun rose. She had the infant tied to her front now, along with two young boys in tow, maybe five and eight years of age.

They all had packs tied to their backs, *chafiyeks* around their necks. The littlest one also carried a stout walking stick.

"I am Seydat. We are going to Hayalevi," she announced.

Trulliç nodded, still not completely surprised. He considered the young woman in front of him. She'd not lived an easy life. Her hands showed strength and wear. She wore the same clothes from the day before, a plain blue tunic over a full black skirt. Clean but faded and patched, hand-me-downs from someone.

A warm spot grabbed Trulliç's attention. There, between her breasts, hung a teardrop shaped piece of glass. She'd strung it on a piece of leather. Though he couldn't see it, he still knew that it matched his own horseshoe, clear glass with gold and green stripes running through it.

Curious, he looked more carefully at the children. Tucked into their packs were small glass balls. Only the infant didn't carry his sign. Trulliç felt no connection to the baby, either. Was the boy too young? Or was it something else?

Seydat appeared to be waiting for Trulliç to say something. Finally, he nodded. "I would be honored to have you," he said seriously. "Though there isn't much there, yet," he warned.

That made Seydat smile. "Yet," she told him. "But there will be."

Trulliç wasn't sure what made her so certain. He was willing to believe her, however.

"Ah, just you?" Trulliç asked, unsure how to delicately inquire about her lack of husband.

"Just us," Seydat said, raising her chin defiantly.

Obviously not a story he was going to get anytime soon.

"That's good!" he said enthusiastically. "I can—"

Another pair of villagers walked up and stood next to Seydat. They were older people, stubborn and strong. "We would go to Hayalevi as well," they announced.

"All right," Trulliç said, surprised. He'd felt no strong connection to this older couple, though they both carried his emblem. They hadn't walked with him the day before, though he wasn't certain how he knew that.

Throughout the morning, more people arrived at the tavern, until Trulliç had a group of eighteen adults, seven teenagers, and five children, all ready to go with him. Some had come with goats, chickens, and sheep.

Trulliç honestly wasn't sure how he was going to feed all these people. How would they occupy themselves? His city wasn't ready yet!

He wasn't about to turn anyone back, though he warned them all about how the city was still in the process of coming alive.

Close to noon, Trulliç felt as though all those who had planned to come had already shown up. Anyone else would have to make their own way to Hayalevi.

Trulliç marched back to the foothills with the group strung out behind him. More villagers had joined them, though they weren't planning on making the entire trip.

Would this sort of parade happen everywhere he went?

Hopefully, over the years people would get more used to seeing him and would treat him with less formality.

Trulliç gathered the group of people who would accompany him into a tight pack, standing closely together.

"Ready?" Trulliç asked them solemnly.

They nodded as one.

Trulliç reached for the thread of connection he felt with every person and wrapped them all tightly around his hand. He picked up the animals, too, collecting them together.

Then he called up a great cloud of sand, sliding it under their feet.

As one, they all took off, gliding toward their new home. Trulliç felt his heart might burst with joy. He had his people! Or at least a few, at any rate.

It didn't matter that most of them were poor or didn't have families.

More would come.

Trulliç settled everyone on the main floor of his tower while he went out to build the rest of his city. The travelers were all glassy-eyed. He wasn't sure why. They seemed shocked to be there. Or maybe it was because his city only contained the single tower, along with the fountain and the altar.

Trulliç strode from his tower, determined. Then he faltered and stopped. Looked around the great flat plane.

What should he build first? He saw what his city would eventually become. But what buildings should he start with? Who should he build for first?

He wanted to build something for Seydat and her children. He couldn't see what, though. What she would want. She should be first. But he couldn't imagine what she wanted.

He turned back toward the tower, only to find Seydat walking toward him. She didn't roll her eyes at him, though that was the feeling he got from her. She'd been the first to recover from their journey, instructing her children to get more water for everyone from the black stone fountain just outside the tower.

"What do you want for a house?" Trulliç asked.

Now Seydat did roll her eyes at him. "You must build the temples first," she instructed Trulliç. "And the fountains and the wells. Then let the other structures come."

Why did she insist on that? Trulliç wasn't sure. However, he did know that his tower hadn't been complete until he'd built the temple to Serrat/Serril.

Grateful for the instruction, Trulliç started raising temples.

He couldn't place the gods too close together—they'd be jealous of one another. He also couldn't make one temple better than the others. As he envisioned the buildings, he realized that all of them needed to be humble places. Intimate. The temples he built were merely altars for the most part. The people closest to them would maintain them. Not priests.

Eventually priests would come. And he'd have to build them houses and their own altars as well.

Trulliç walked toward where he envisioned the market square, wanting to start there. He wanted his people to be prosperous. So he first built the temple to Innis, the god of fertility, in the south western corner of the square. He carved a great spear over the doorway so Innis's followers would know him. Dark stones made up the temple walls, a dark and sober place, fit for a dark and somber god.

Trulliç set up the temple to Enkat on the opposite corner of the market. She was much loved of storytellers and scholars, as well as farmers and shepherds, as her dance brought much needed rain. Trulliç carved her altar out of the far wall of her temple, while he left the middle of the room open, the ground covered with fine, fresh sand, so dancers and performers could perform as well as worship there.

The temple to Xannil was farther away, on the eastern edge of Hayalevi. It took Trulliç a moment to realize that he'd placed it exactly where the sun would touch the great plain first most days during the summer. The sun god's temple was another dark place as he was a jealous god, hiding away Enkat his wife so the rains didn't come. Trulliç built a small alley with open lean-tos next to the temple, where fortune tellers and dream readers would come to ply their trade.

Barzhat got her temple in the north of the city. The goddess of death's altar had a light, airy feeling to it as Trulliç punched holes through the roof, opening it to the sky. It, too, had a fine sand floor for people to dance on, practicing the steps they'd give for the goddess one day.

Onnet's temple drew Trulliç to the west. He meant to make it like all the others, but the stone walls formed in the shape of a horseshoe and he chose not to fight them. He made cozy seats for crones to sit and rest their bones, as well as places where young, pregnant women could come and gossip. It was one of the few buildings he added colors to, green and orange stones lining the edges of the main doorway.

When Trulliç finished, he felt the pattern of the altars around him. They weren't balanced. The temples to the east and west held those edges of the city. The market square held down the southwest corner. His tower and Serrat/Serril's temple sat directly in the center of Hayalevi.

But he needed one more sacred place. To the east and north, to balance the marketplace temples.

Trulliç let his feet guide him, wandering across the river, past his towers, and east. A small building pushed at him. Smaller than the temple to Serrat/Serril, than all the other temples. About the size of the altar Trulliç had visited first as part of his manhood journey so many years before.

Riyune suddenly appeared at his side. The dog pushed up against his leg so Trulliç could see better.

A small, dark spot appeared on the sand in front of Trulliç. He felt the stones under the ground, calling to him. They wanted to be freed.

Trulliç raised his glass horseshoe and tugged at the rocks he felt there. With a sigh of relief, the stones pushed out of the cold ground, forming together, basking in the sunlight.

Trulliç knew that no matter the time of day or how hot it got, the air inside the littlest temple would always feel cool. The rocks themselves remained rough, as if scalloped by the wind and nothing else.

The temple bore no mark. No symbol to tell people who they worshipped there.

There wasn't even an altar inside, just a void where an altar had once stood.

Trulliç turned his back on the temple to Forit after he raised it, refusing to walk into it.

However, he knew that even though he'd never visited the place, that wouldn't matter. The temple, and the missing altar, would always haunt his dreams.

The rest of the houses came easily after that: squat one-story rambling buildings for the older people, ones with more stories for the younger people. Trulliç built a shared compound for the goats, the sheep keeping to themselves. Yards with stone fences for the chickens. The huts all had glass windows. Trulliç found the shapes inside of himself, square and solid, the walls mostly red and golden. Rooms divided onto other rooms, giving people more space, more privacy.

He also discovered that trees came with the buildings, tall date trees and palms, fig trees and cottonwood. He didn't know that they lived under the earth with the stones, but they shot up as he constructed the buildings and boulevards. *Meslit* thorns came, too, along with bushes and flowers. Even tough grasses sprang up near the waterways and at the base of the fountains.

Fields would come soon. They'd never bear that much, but there would be enough grain to feed the few who lived in Hayalevi now.

Trade routes needed to be established, and soon.

After he'd settled everyone, he came back to his tower to find Seydat and her children waiting for him. She'd prepared tea for him, brewed exactly how he liked it, sweet and strong.

"Thank you," Trulliç said, accepting a cup gratefully. "I need to build you a home," he said seriously after he'd allowed the tea to clear his throat and refresh him.

Seydat smiled at him and shook her head. "You need someone to keep you organized," she said seriously. "To greet your guests, settle them into the city when you're away on business."

Trulliç blinked, surprised. "I do?" he asked. He had never thought he'd need an assistant. Though that was what he'd been to Atça in many ways.

But Gaadiwala had been a tiny village, maybe one hundred families.

Hayalevi would grow to many times that size, given time.

"I don't know how to pay you," Trulliç said seriously, giving voice to his greatest fear. "I can raise houses, build fountains for the oasis water, even grow some desert plants. But I cannot create coins out of the air."

Seydat nodded. "You can give me a place to live, a purpose for my life. An education for my children so that they can have a better existence. Coin will come as the people do, paying you for your glass and goods."

"All right," Trulliç said slowly. He hadn't expected anyone to pay him for creating glass goods. He paused, then added, "You will have to see to your own food. I…I'm not going to be hungry. Often." He gulped, then finally admitted, "Ever."

Seydat seemed surprised at that. "You don't need to eat?" she asked, incredulous.

"I don't think so," Trulliç told her. "I'm never hungry." He had had a few bites to eat while at Brugar's tavern, out of courtesy, but for the most part all he'd had was tea.

"Then it won't matter that we don't have much coin presently," Seydat told him firmly. "Now, you need to build me a small room, off the side of this tower."

Trulliç made to push himself to standing, then he shook his head and settled back down.

"No," he said, surprised at himself. Most of Seydat's ideas had been correct. He was more than willing to admit that. "You need a separate place. A place of honor."

She shook her head but he held up his hand to stop her before she spoke. "You are a single woman with three children. You need a space for your family that is your own. Apart from your position." He didn't add that she also needed to be away from him. As much as he loved having other people around, he still needed the ability to be alone.

Seydat tilted her head to the side and looked at Trulliç with disbelief. "You are naïve," she said softly. "My association with you is my status."

"For now," Trulliç said. "But you will have your own place among my people."

Seydat shook her head but only said, "We'll see."

* * *

When Trulliç finished building Seydat's house—a large building with two floors, directly next to his tower—he insisted that she and her children go and stay there while he rested.

Trulliç wasn't tired. The sun and the sand continued to energize him. He just needed some quiet. He walked all the way to the top of his tower and looked proudly over Hayalevi. True, there weren't many buildings there. But he'd add more as more people came.

The sun hung low in the western sky, the coolness of the evening already creeping in. Trulliç breathed in the night, trying to calm his rising anger. The rage had slowly haunted him all day, growing greater as he'd created his town.

Why hadn't Atça done more for the people in Gaadiwala? Was he actually that weak of a magician? Yerkoyliç had held all of Çandekili in his palm. He hadn't built all of the buildings there—the town had existed before he'd been born—but he'd strengthened them. Made them taller and richer.

Yerkoyliç had still made Çandekili a place to be proud of. And it had died with him. Trulliç knew that the stones he raised would stay standing even after his death.

What was wrong with Atça? Was he really that miserly with his power?

And why hadn't Atça told Trulliç that he was the desert magician? Why had Atça lied to him all those years?

Trulliç had never dreamed of the desert as a young boy, though magicians always dreamt of their true homes. Why had Trulliç never seen this place?

Had Atça put *agafi* in Trulliç's water?

Trulliç remembered first walking the desert when he'd been twelve. The water skins had been filled with water from Atça's sweet well.

He remembered how the cavern that had found him had insisted that he dump those skins out, fill them with pure water instead.

Had the skins been full of *agafi*? Was that why Trulliç had gone wandering that first time across the sands? Had almost died?

The rage built like a summer storm, quick and overwhelming.

Trulliç cast himself from the top of his tower out onto the sands, heading directly north. He became a howling wind, swirling up and up, taller even than his tower. Dust, heat, and small rocks flew like arrows from his path. Lightning crackled around him. The smell of death flowed with him.

Why? *Why?* WHY?

Trulliç howled and cried as he raced across the desert. The heat of the sun couldn't compare to the white hot fury of his rage.

He'd been lied to. Tricked. Fooled. His entire life.

Atça still lied about him, Trulliç felt certain.

Hell, Atça had hired Nadeem to *kill* Trulliç.

Enough.

Trulliç didn't have to suffer Atça any longer.

He would go and confront his former mentor.

Now.

INTERLUDE

TRULLIÇ BLEW DOWN ATÇA'S DOOR, his desert winds howling, raging around him. He stomped into the front entrance way, sneering at the wood there.

He remembered when he used to think that Atça was the richest person alive.

The hallway, the house, the entire town, seemed so closed in. Trulliç couldn't imagine ever living someplace ever again when he couldn't see the stars.

"Atça!" Trulliç yelled. "Get out here!" The entire house shook with the power of his voice.

Atça walked out of the darkened hallway leading to the rest of his house. He wore his typical black and blue striped tunic, with a shirt so white it looked like bleached bones. His pants were solid black, but he had bare feet instead of house slippers. He stood tall and proud before Trulliç, his dark eyes glaring.

"How dare you enter my house like this!" Atça roared. "You are not the master here."

"You know better than to challenge me," Trulliç warned him.

Atça suddenly looked uncertain.

"I found my home," Trulliç said. "It *is* Qaenev. The entire desert." Trulliç couldn't help but still feel wonder. The sands. The rocks. The hidden places. The oasis. His new city. All of it.

"I know," Atça said sourly.

"You knew? You knew that my home was the desert? Why? Why didn't you tell me?" Trulliç demanded.

That was the real reason why he'd come to confront his old mentor, his tormentor. To demand answers about how Trulliç had been trained. The lies Atça had maintained.

"It wasn't my place," Atça maintained steadily. "You needed to find out on your own."

"You kept me weak," Trulliç accused Atça. "Tied to your side."

"I kept you alive," Atça told him. "How do you think the emperor would have felt about a magician who claimed the entire desert? He would have had you killed outright when you were a babe."

"You did try to kill me," Trulliç said. He believed Nadeem's oath. That Atça had hired her. Thank all the gods that she'd broken it.

Atça shrugged. "You were no longer useful," he said.

"Malleable," Trulliç countered.

Atça shrugged again.

"I never dreamed of the desert when I was younger," Trulliç said. He remembered the first time he'd walked the desert when he'd been twelve. The vision from the stream, making him pour out what remained of Atça's sweet water, the flagons Atça had filled from his well. "Did you feed me *agafi*? All the while I was younger? So I'd never dream of the desert?"

That was the one question Trulliç dreaded asking.

The one he knew he must. Had his mentor fed Trulliç a potion that would give him dreamless sleep?

Atça pressed his lips together for a moment as if he wouldn't answer. Finally, though, he nodded. "I did."

"Why?" Trulliç asked. He hated how his voice cracked, how he sounded so heartbroken.

Atça had betrayed him. From the very start.

"I knew you were a desert magician. *The* desert magician. If you dreamed too young of the desert, you wouldn't have survived," Atça said. He sounded as though he was trying to be reasonable. "Tell me. How overwhelmed you might have been if you'd started dreaming of the entire desert when you were seven. Trying to take it all in."

Trulliç paused. Could he have handled it?

"Your mother came to me when you were that age," Atça said. "Told me of your nightmares. You weren't sleeping. I decided to let you live and to merely stop your dreams, so you wouldn't wander into the desert when you were too young and be consumed."

"You should have stopped giving me the *agafi* sooner," Trulliç told him. "Before I walked the desert the first time."

"You were too fanciful. Seeing magic. Living in poetry," Atça sneered. "How could I have known?"

"You poisoned my water the first time I walked the desert," Trulliç said.

Atça shook his head. "No. I merely gave you much more of the *agafi* so you might survive."

Trulliç bit his lips together. Atça told the truth as far as he could tell. His old mentor probably just hadn't realized how the extra *agafi* would affect Trulliç or make him wander the desert in the midday sun.

"Why did you keep me alive?" Trulliç plaintively. It was the one last question he had. Since Atça had seemed to know just how powerful Trulliç would get one day, why hadn't he done his duty to the emperor and killed Trulliç outright when he was just a babe? Defenseless?

Atça gave a barking laugh. "You will go after the desert heart on your own one day," he predicted. "Keep it. Use it." He shook his head. "I had hoped, when you'd been younger, that you might have brought it to your old mentor out of gratitude."

Trulliç blinked, surprised. *That* had been why Atça had kept him alive? So that he might gain the full power of the desert heart and use it himself?

Of course, Atça was that greedy. He always kept all of the power, the wealth of Gaadiwala to himself.

"What is the desert heart? Really?" Trulliç asked. He didn't believe that it was Forit's heart, still intertwined with the darkness from before the creation of the world.

But Atça just laughed again and shook his head. "You'll have to find out for yourself. If you can get it before the emperor kills you."

"How much does the emperor know about me?" Trulliç demanded.

"He knows you're no longer under my control," Atça sneered. "Not since you killed Yerkoyliç I've informed him of how dangerous you are, how you're no longer loyal."

"But it was *your* idea to kill Yerkoyliç! Your plan!" Trulliç said, his anger building.

He never would have left Gaadiwala if Atça hadn't given him the assignment in the first place.

Atça gave him a wintery smile. "That might be viewed as a mistake," he said haughtily. "Or as an opportunity. No one will ever believe you that it wasn't your idea, that you weren't so desperate to find your own home that you thought you'd try to take Çandekili first." His smile grew colder. "Oh yes. The emperor has heard all about you by now. I've made sure of it."

"It was your last mistake," Trulliç said.

He understood much better now the relationship between a people and their magician. How strong or weak they could become. He had his own city. Not many people, but they were coming.

Gaadiwala would only be slightly worse off without Atça. But in many ways, they'd be stronger as well without this greedy monster constantly bleeding them dry. He'd be happy to make his case in front of any judge, or pay any fine.

From his side, Trulliç drew a handful of sand out from a small bag and cast it at Atça.

He'd also learned a lot from the land box. Like how to carry enough desert with him when he left.

The sand flew directly into Atça's face before he could defend himself. He choked on it, falling back into the darkened hallway. Hacking and dying loudly.

Trulliç left before the house collapsed around him.

He would spend a short time here, and talk to the people of Gaadiwala, tell them what had happened, what was to come.

Then he had to get back to the desert.

To be ready to greet the emperor's soldiers when they arrived.

CHAPTER SIX

NADEEM

NADEEM GLIDED ACROSS THE SAND on her new-found power, like a stone skipping across the water. She could maintain her speed only for a short while, then she would land and walk for a while.

She knew this was how Trulliç traveled, only he never had to stop. It filled her with both joy and dread. She loved the freedom of how she moved but feared what it meant that she was becoming.

As Nadeem slowed, she felt her pack pushing at her, tugging her back toward earth.

The only thing in her pack that felt heavy when she ran was the snake-headed stick she carried. The pull of it was what slowed her down. Its shadow needed to touch the ground.

Nadeem stopped and looked around. The main body of the desert lay to her right. She still skirted the edges, following an old oasis trail. Summer had already come to the desert, the short spring exhausted. Small thorns and bushes lined the path she followed. She would have to get out of the sun soon before it reached its zenith. The air carried just a hint of water, but mostly just iron-touched baked rocks.

After taking a surprisingly sweet mouthful of water from one of the skins she carried with her, Nadeem took off again. She resented every time she had to stop, however, she couldn't leave the stick behind. Not like she'd left her sweet camel Banut, giving her to Aunt Parayat to sell in exchange for the goods she carried.

The next oasis was just ahead. Nadeem would push herself to reach there before full day. Then rest until evening and travel some more.

It wouldn't take her long to reach Trulliç's city—Hayalevi. If she could somehow sell how she traveled, she knew merchants such as Levent would buy her services in a heartbeat. Being able to cross the desert quickly would put him at a great advantage.

Then again, Levant might choose to travel slowly, to give fate the chance to offer him treats. If he moved too fast, he might miss something, something important.

Nadeem didn't think she'd miss anything. Except possibly Trulliç if she didn't keep hurrying along.

She had to get to him before the emperor or his guards did.

Though she didn't know how she knew, she still felt it in her bones.

The emperor was on his way.

<hr>

Nadeem paused on the slight slope that lay just to the west of Hayalevi. She whistled quietly to herself.

It had been a little more than a month since Nadeem had last seen Trulliç. He'd been *busy*.

Neighborhoods took up every corner of the town. Empty spaces still lay between them. In her mind's eye, Nadeem could already see the buildings crowding out the open areas.

A tower stood in the center of the city. Nadeem knew that would be Trulliç's tower. It was the highest building in the city. Nadeem suspected it always would be. Even the guard towers that Trulliç would eventually build wouldn't be as tall.

The water course she followed ran deep and smooth, the water like black glass. She figured she'd imagined that there was actually glass at the bottom of the river, though now, seeing the city and all the glass windows, maybe she had actually sensed it.

Dawn was just approaching, long fingers of light stretching their way from the hills to the city below. People already stirred, and the smell of fresh flatbread wafted toward her. To the south of the city lay fields of grain, small but fruitful. Closer in stood an orchard.

None of this had been here before Trulliç, Nadeem was certain.

But then, he hadn't known he was a desert magician.

She could only shake her head as she made her way down the hill.

T he door to Trulliç's tower stood open. However, a large black rock stood just inside the opening, a guard stone. Nadeem recognized it as similar to the one that had blocked the opening to the cavern that had found her, protected and healed her.

The stone felt cool and smooth to her fingertips, like black glass, though she could see the pits in the rock.

"Hello?" Nadeem called as she stuck her head around the corner.

A young woman sat nursing an infant in the corner. An older woman sat beside her, spinning idly on a drop spindle. They both wore tunics that were a surprising gray color, like soft clouds, though the young woman had green and gold ribbons tied into her long braid, and the older woman wore a *chafiyek* made out of the same colors.

The room itself was plain and bigger than Nadeem expected, easily able to hold two dozen people. The glass windows had been tinted with blue to keep the bright sunlight out. A pile of pillows lay stacked in the corners, along with some rolled up rugs, ready to be pulled out when guests arrived. Glass lamps hung from the ceiling, making the room quite bright.

Tall, evenly spaced stones made up the walls, like bricks made by giants, each about the height of Nadeem and three times as wide as she was tall. They were the same red-gold as most of the city, as if baked out of burnt sand.

"Hello, traveler," the young woman said, nodding her welcome. "Please, come sit with us. Rest after your long journey." She indicated the spare guest rug sitting beside her.

The older woman stared at Nadeem. "I know you," she said quietly.

Nadeem blinked, startled. "Do you?" she asked, challenging, as she stepped further into the room.

The older woman gasped quietly when she saw Nadeem's mangled cheek. "I do. I served you tea in Gaadiwala, at the Horseshoe Tavern. You and your two…sisters."

Nadeem held herself still. This woman *did* look familiar. Nadeem remembered her now. Her face appeared slightly less bitter than it had, her look a touch more friendly.

And she still shared the same bones as Trulliç. A relative, probably his mother.

"I am merely a traveler," Nadeem told them clearly. She was no longer a star sister.

"You are still welcome," the older woman told her. She even gave Nadeem a small smile, though it looked as though the action was unfamiliar to her. "Come. Sit. Rest. Would you like water? Tea? Food?"

Nadeem knelt on the blue-and-black braided rug beside the women. It was awkward, but she didn't want to remove her pack. Not yet.

"Water, tea, would be welcome," she said. "And possibly some flatbread. Nothing fancy."

The young woman finished suckling her babe and pulled him with a sleepy protest from her breast. "Not fancy is what we do here," she said with a smile as she tied the infant to her chest. "I'll let you two catch up," she added with a wink as she briskly walked from the room.

The older woman tilted her head to one side to study Nadeem. "How did you find Hayalevi?"

"It was in my dreams," Nadeem told her truthfully. "But I also need to see Trulliç. I bring grave news."

The woman nodded. "He will return before the end of the day. He strengthens the borders of the desert against the coming of the emperor's guards," she said frankly. "I am Myrizhah," she added.

"Nadeem," she said. "Thank you for your hospitality," she added.

Myrizhah gave her a soft laugh. "It isn't much. We're still fighting to make ends meet, to have enough bread and food for everyone. Water is plentiful. And glass. Not much else."

Nadeem nodded. "I saw the buildings as I came through the town, from the west. Did Trulliç make all the glass?"

"He did," Myrizhah said proudly. "As well as raised all the buildings, the roads, the trees and the fields."

"Trulliç has finally come into his own, then," Nadeem said.

Myrizhah laughed softly and shook her head. "No. He is still young.

Still learning. If he can survive the next few years, then maybe…" Her voice faded and she looked into the distance.

Nadeem looked puzzled at Myrizhah. "Maybe?" she asked softly.

"Don't pay attention to an old woman's ramblings," Myrizhah said. "Did you meet my son when you were in Gaadiwala?"

"Yes," Nadeem said.

The other woman came back with a tea service unlike any Nadeem had seen before. The cups were polished glass, clear with gold rims and green bottoms. Stray traces of color ran through them. The teapot, as well, had been made from glass.

When the younger woman set the tray down, Nadeem realized everything was made of glass: the tray, the plates, the holders for the salt and lard, the small bowl with picked onions, even the knife.

"Fine work," Nadeem said as she picked up the knife. Though the glass pieces would be difficult to transport, they would bring a hefty price at any of the markets.

"It comes from Trulliç's heart," Myrizhah said. "But it's cold."

The women exchanged a look. They both worried about him.

Could the younger woman be Trulliç's wife? No, she probably was married to someone else, probably a relative. Trulliç could create a town but not a babe in merely a month's time.

She felt uncomfortable at the touch of relief that came over her when she realized Trulliç was still unattached.

All the women ate a bit, drinking a fine citrus tea and chatting about the rains that they needed, the way people arrived in the city every day, and Nadeem's journey across the sand.

When Nadeem had eaten her fill, Myrizhah asked, "Do you need a room? Or would you like to set up a tent near the market?"

She clearly intended for Nadeem to be on her way, no matter what news she said she carried.

Nadeem thought for a moment. "I need to see Trulliç," she said softly.

Myrizhah shook her head. "I'll tell him the moment he arrives—"

Nadeem took her pack from her back. She pulled out the emperor's snake-headed stick, then walked with it to the edge of the door.

It tugged at her. It didn't like Trulliç's tower. It wanted out.

Too bad.

The guard stone stood just inside the entrance to the tower. Nadeem placed the stick on the far side of the stone, then walked back into the room.

A whirlwind sprang up in front of the guard stone. The sand on the floor circled up in small sandstorms. The smell of baked rocks and harsh storm winds flowed into the room.

When everything died down, Trulliç stood there. Riyune stood beside him.

"Nadeem!" Trulliç said excitedly, taking two steps toward her.

Then he stopped. Frowned.

Turned back toward the door and stuck his head around the guard stone, staring at the stick waiting ominously for him.

"What is that evil thing?" he asked, his tone grown as cold as a winter storm.

"A present from the emperor," Nadeem told him. "Gifted to the man I was assigned to kill."

Without warning, Nadeem found herself carried to the top of the tower. She knew steps flowed beneath her feet. She couldn't have stopped, though. Nothing in her training left her prepared for this type of magic.

At the clear opening on the top of the tower, Nadeem caught her breath and surged to her feet. She planted herself firmly in the bright sunlight. If she could have, she would have pushed roots down into the earth so that Trulliç could *never* do that to her again.

Trulliç stood beside her, glowering. The stick floated in midair, off the edge of the tower. Riyune had evidently wisely stayed below.

"Don't," Nadeem told Trulliç. He obviously intended to blow it into a million pieces.

"Why not?" he asked, frost coating his tone.

Nadeem nodded. She'd hoped that by finding, and founding, his city, that Trulliç would have spent his rage.

She'd been wrong. He'd grown much, much more angry.

Maybe she should have killed him when she'd had the chance.

"Did you know I was coming?" Nadeem challenged him. "Did you feel my footprints across the desert?"

Trulliç slowly shook his head.

Nadeem marched over to where the stick still hovered, poised for its destruction. She boldly reached out and grasped it, ignoring how slippery the wood still felt, how she was no longer on stable ground but reaching far over the edge of the tower. She still gripped it, determined, off balance, her own anger building.

No matter how well trained she was, Trulliç could still send her tumbling to her death in an instant. And the idiot just might do it.

"And now can you find me? With senses other than your eyes?" she asked. She tugged on the stick, trying to bring it closer. To get a better stance.

It stubbornly stayed floating in the air exactly where Trulliç had placed it.

Trulliç narrowed his eyes at her. He blasted sand at her, but it slid around her, the edges of the storm caressing her.

Nadeem held on.

"But how?" Trulliç finally asked her, his anger fading. "Why does that hide you? Why can't I reach you when you're touching it?"

Nadeem shrugged. "I don't know. But do you think you could let go of your anger long enough to help me figure this out?"

Trulliç blushed, his tanned skin growing much darker. "I can," he said softly. He drew the stick back across the edge of the tower, letting go of it so that Nadeem could take its weight again. "I'm sorry," he said.

Nadeem nodded. That would have to do for now.

He'd never survive the upcoming battles if he lost himself in rage, however.

And Nadeem wasn't sure that she had the time to teach him.

The young woman appeared at the top of the stairs after a few moments. "Tea?" she asked Trulliç.

"Please, Seydat," he said, still staring hard at the stick Nadeem held.

"Is that your wife?" Nadeem asked after the woman ducked back into the tower. Nadeem knew she was flouting custom by asking so directly.

She also figured Trulliç wouldn't mind.

"No," Trulliç said, still distracted. "She's my assistant. And you met my mother, too. Myrizhah?"

"Ah," Nadeem said. The other woman downstairs. That explained much. Both the woman's previous bitterness and her current worry.

Trulliç reached one hand out to touch the walking stick, then hesitated. "May I?" he asked, finally looking up at her. Then he blinked.

"What happened to your face?" he asked. His own mien instantly grew dark and stormy.

"I am no longer a star sister," Nadeem said, raising her chin defiantly. "I am merely a traveler now."

"Who did that to you?" Trulliç said, the storm approaching again all too quickly.

"I did." Nadeem subtly widened her stance in case Trulliç decided to blast her.

"You did that to yourself? Why?" Trulliç asked. He seemed truly confused.

Nadeem wasn't sure how to answer him. He was at the heart of her failure. "I can't live by their oaths anymore," was all she replied.

"Are you here to kill me?" he asked, tilting his head to one side.

Nadeem gave a bitter laugh. "As if I could." Though Nadeem had never met another land magician, she knew Trulliç was the strongest of them all.

"Atça is dead," Trulliç told her. "I killed him."

Then why are you still so angry? Nadeem didn't ask that. She suspected Trulliç didn't know.

"So you have no oath to fulfill, not in regards to me," he boasted.

"That isn't how it works," Nadeem said. "Killing the oath maker doesn't erase the oath."

"Not even if both parties are dead?" Trulliç asked softly.

Nadeem couldn't help but wince. Technically, he was right. She was dead, at least as far as the star sisters were concerned. So was Atça. If he'd never asked another star sister to fulfill the oath…

Still, Nadeem shrugged. "We'll see," she said. No matter what the *kabil* of star sisters might eventually decide, Nadeem still knew what she had done, as well as what she had chosen not to do. Only Barzhat could judge the weight of her deeds.

Trulliç continued to stare at Nadeem's mangled cheek. "You used to have a different aura," he said eventually. "Light blue and pink. Pearlescent. It's changed. There are more colors in it now. More gold and green."

"I am a desert creature," Nadeem told him. "Like you."

Trulliç finally gave her a true smile. "Really?"

Seydat poked her head above the staircase again. "You should come inside, Trulliç," she said. "Make your guest more comfortable," she added sternly.

"Oh. Oh! Sorry," Trulliç said. He seemed chastened. "I am most comfortable outside, in the bright sunlight," he explained. "I do know though, that other people aren't. Please, come with me inside, into the shade, where it's cooler."

Seydat gave him a nod of approval.

Nadeem couldn't help but smile to herself as he escorted her down the stairs.

Trulliç was trying to do the right thing. And it appeared he had some good help.

But there was still so much for him to learn. For him to figure out.

And there wasn't much time.

Nadeem and Trulliç circled each other warily.

They had walked out of the city, past the flat plain and the gravel, onto the sand itself. Night stretched from the east, though the sky in the west still burned orange and red. Stars floated above them. The desert hawks had finished their hunting, their cries fading. Cool breezes floated around them, carrying the sweet smell of dates.

After they'd spent time talking in Trulliç's study, they'd come out here. Trulliç had left the stick in his mother's care, though she'd complained about how slippery the wood felt when she'd touched it. They'd left Riyune behind to guard the stick as well, though the dog had seemed indifferent to the stick.

Nadeem had insisted that they leave the city, though, so she could start training Trulliç how to fight.

Her real intent was to make him learn how to battle without losing his temper.

Generally the first lessons were all about falling. A girl had to learn how to fall without hurting herself.

However, Trulliç didn't have the patience for that. So they'd started immediately with wrestling.

Trulliç's green-and-gold striped tunic already showed his first falls. Though he had a longer reach, he didn't have her training.

Or her speed.

He should have been faster than her out there on the sand. Was he holding himself back? Or did he not know how to apply it? He could run, yes. Skim over the desert faster than a falling hawk. But he couldn't move his arms or hands as fast.

After Nadeem had knocked him on his ass for a third time, she asked in exasperation, "Didn't you have any brothers and sisters? Cousins you fought with?"

Trulliç shook his head. "Only child. I had cousins, but I didn't spend that much time with them. I had lessons with Atça instead."

Even in the dim light, Nadeem could see his expression grow darker.

That was why Trulliç knew the old poems and could recite them. It had been part of his training.

Of course, Atça hadn't considered training the body to be as important as training the mind.

Nadeem easily blocked his next attempt to grab. "What, are you afraid to hit a girl?" she taunted. She slid out of his hold and twisted around him, tripping him so he stumbled.

"No!" Trulliç said. "I could pick you up and throw you to the very edge of the sands with my magic," he growled.

"But if someone got through your magical defenses, you'd be helpless as an infant," Nadeem sneered. "Hell, even a star sister who hadn't had her initiation could kill you."

Trulliç barred his teeth and rushed at her.

Nadeem sidestepped his awkward attempt and spilled him onto the sands again.

"And they will be coming for you," Nadeem told Trulliç. "Not initiates. But trained stars. Ones fanatically dedicated to the emperor. How will you stop them?"

With a roar, Trulliç tried to grab Nadeem. He missed.

"Or do you only fancy yourself a great warrior?" she asked. "Are you still just a boy?"

Nadeem knew the instant before Trulliç grabbed her with his magic that she'd finally pushed him too far. Or at least far enough that he could accidentally kill her.

She suddenly found herself spinning in a whirlwind, abrasive sand cutting her cheek, the wound there sending spikes of pain. The floor of the desert lay far beneath her feet. Cooler winds caressed her.

The storm died down as quickly as it started, the winds silencing themselves. Nadeem found herself poised like a great eagle, ready to plunge to her death.

She opened her arms and closed her eyes, welcoming Barzhat's embrace.

Trulliç's voice sounded right in front of her face. "Why?" he asked plaintively. "Why are you doing this?"

Nadeem opened her eyes. They both floated high above the desert, at least as high as the top of Trulliç's tower. The sands spread below them like a jeweled carpet below her. She hadn't expected the sand to sparkle in the night. Or was that part of Trulliç's magic? She smelled the water from the oasis trail leading into Hayalevi. Felt the far border of the desert fading into hills to the south. Tasted the cool sweat of her fear.

"You must learn to control yourself," Nadeem told Trulliç. "If I can get you to lose your temper so easily and make mistakes, so will the emperor's guards."

Trulliç sighed. "I'm not sure how," he admitted. "I go racing out across the desert almost every night. A storm of death. Trying to blow it away."

Nadeem nodded. "Does that help?"

"Sometimes," Trulliç replied. "Sometimes not."

That didn't surprise Nadeem. "You must face your anger," she told him, "and defeat it. Or it will destroy you and everything you've built."

"I told you. I already killed Atça," Trulliç said darkly.

"But that didn't help," Nadeem pointed out. "You need to overcome his lies."

"How?" Trulliç asked, sounding much younger than his eighteen years.

Nadeem's own anger surfaced. She had her own failures to face. The lies she'd been told to overcome. "I don't know," she told him coldly. "Just do it. Or we're all lost."

Trulliç nodded sadly. Slowly, they began to float back down to earth. But not straight down. Nadeem felt as though she was a feather floating on a breeze, drifting slowly to the ground. She found her breath catch, and her heart filled with wonder at the gentle journey.

Trulliç landed a few feet away from her, looking back toward the city. "What will happen if I fail?" he asked.

"Your city will be blasted back into the sands. Your people killed. Your name will be used as a curse," Nadeem said. "Or worse. The entire world will fall when the emperor makes his bid to become a god."

The gibbering darkness of her visions unleashed on the world. Those who could stop it becoming corrupted by it instead. All the light and goodness destroyed.

"Why are you here?" Trulliç demanded. "Really? What is your mission from your aunts?"

Nadeem sighed. But it was easier talking to him this way, listening to the quiet of the desert, feeling the peace of the night, rather than talking in earnest to one another.

"Aunt Parayat said I must stop the emperor," Nadeem said.

"Kill him?" Trulliç asked sharply.

"Just stop him," Nadeem said. "I've yet to kill anyone."

Trulliç gave a bitter laugh. "And I've killed three men so far. With more to come, I'm sure."

The quiet came over them again. "We will stop him," he assured her. "One way or another."

Nadeem couldn't help but smile. "Or die trying."

"May your dance for Barzhat be short," Trulliç said, giving her the traditional reply.

"Yours too," Nadeem said. "Should we go back to the city?"

Trulliç nodded. "Sure. I want to—" He paused. Stiffened.

Grew angry again.

"What is it?" Nadeem asked.

Trulliç looked over at her. His eyes burned like hard diamonds. Sand whirled around his feet.

"The emperor's guards. They're here."

CHAPTER SEVEN

TRULLIÇ

DESPITE THE GROWING NIGHT, TRULLIÇ still went immediately to "greet" the emperor's guards.

He knew he wasn't at full strength. Had the guards arrived at the border after sunset in order to take advantage of that? Or was it just a coincidence?

Trulliç didn't believe in that sort of luck. Particularly not where the emperor was concerned.

He brought Nadeem with him, in part because she'd insisted, but also because he hoped she would keep him from doing something stupid.

Like just killing all of the guards offhand. Because he could.

Trulliç wasn't sure why the guards approached the desert from the west. Surely it would have been faster to approach them from the direct north? That was where Atayurtkah lay, the emperor's grand city. When would the emperor send people from the city? It had been a little more than a month since Trulliç had founded his city.

Maybe these guards had been stationed to the north, in Lydea, and had sailed down from there.

Trulliç remembered Yerkoyliç's dismay when the magic in his town's wall hadn't automatically reacted to Trulliç's presence. At the time, Trulliç had assumed it was because he was such a poor magician.

Now he wondered if his own magical power had been so great it had overwhelmed Yerkoyliç's defenses without Trulliç even realizing it.

However, the emperor's guards had set off the wards that Trulliç had been strengthening all around the border of the desert. As Trulliç and Nadeem neared where the guards stood, Trulliç couldn't help his smug smile.

Two dozen guards stood just past the border of the desert, shuffling their feet uneasily.

In front of them, on the desert side of the border, floated a large array of glass balls. They varied in size from the length of Trulliç's pinky to larger than his head. Colors ranged as well—from midnight black to clear, deep violet to brilliant yellow.

The glass balls all floated about the same height as a man's head. Anytime a guard shifted, the balls did as well, looming and threatening so the guards couldn't cross into the desert.

The balls didn't form an impenetrable barrier. They did act as a warning, telling any visitor that they were about to step into a magical place owned by a powerful magician.

Now that Trulliç was here, he could make the balls explode, and the glass shards would automatically aim for the eyes of the guards, blinding them. One of the bigger balls could kill a man by driving deadly glass spikes into his heart.

The guards all wore similar outfits, the leather of their chest plates dyed red with a great golden emblem in the center of each. It took Trulliç a moment to realize that it was a snake's scale—the symbol of the emperor.

They wore short leather aprons that hung down to their knees. Underneath, depending on the season, they wore either long wool trousers or shorter, lighter weight, cropped cotton pants. Their sandals were solid leather, hearty and well worn.

They all had shields tied to their backs, but they didn't carry the same weapon. Some had bows, others had knives and swords, still others had whips and long pikes with wicked bayonets. They stood as a unit despite their different fighting implements. They'd probably trained together for a long while.

Trulliç touched ground inside the border so the mass of floating glass balls stood between him and the guards. Nadeem stood at his side. Just behind him, Trulliç felt the white streak that was Riyune, racing to meet them.

Riyune would probably be upset that he'd had to get there on his own. But he wasn't about to miss out on all the fun.

Trulliç stepped forward, causing the balls to clear a space for him in the center while forming a more solid line on either side. "I am Trulliç," he announced. "This is my desert."

Nadeem stepped forward as well, standing at his left side, while Riyune appeared at his right. They both bristled at the group, strong and capable.

Trulliç was not alone. It was a novel feeling, one he wasn't used to. It made him feel both proud as well as uncomfortable.

An older guard stepped forward, though keeping to his side of the border. "I am Marius," he said. "I am the head of the local garrison at Erdinet, come to meet the desert magician, at the command of the emperor."

Marius was obviously from the northern kingdom of Lydae. He had a bulbous nose and wore his hair in the longer, northern style. Though it was too dim to see clearly, Trulliç would bet that Marius had light-colored eyes. He stood a head shorter than the guards around him, but he looked solid and well-muscled.

Trulliç paused, considering. Erdinet was a seaport, located on one of the southern most islands of the kingdom of Lydae. Had the soldiers sailed from there? If so, then their approach of the desert from the west would make more sense.

But why had the *Padisha-i-Ghazi* sent *this* group of soldiers? There had to be something special about them, a reason why the emperor would trust them with contacting the new desert magician.

Trulliç peered more closely at the men. They seemed hardened, more weary and bitter than the soldiers he'd seen passing through Gaadiwala. Their weapons were worn, well used.

"Welcome to my desert," Trulliç said belatedly. "I am honored by your presence."

"We have talked with villagers along the oasis trail. More than one has dreamed of your great city, Hayalevi," Marius continued. "We would like to see it, to report to the emperor of the wonderful addition to his empire."

"Ah," Trulliç said. He knew that the emperor's guards would come to investigate his city. But what did they truly expect to find?

"You will be welcome there," Trulliç said. He waved his hand, causing the glass balls to sink directly back under the sand, set to warn of the next travelers.

"Are all to be greeted thusly?" Marius questioned as he and his men stepped across the border.

Trulliç pushed his senses out, focusing on the men's steps, seeking their feet.

The guards didn't have the same feeling as the cane did, that void or darkness.

But there was something…shifty…about them.

There was much more to this group of guards than what met the eye.

Trulliç was going to have to keep a very good watch on them, using all his senses.

"Only large groups will awaken the desert's natural defenses," Nadeem said, stepping forward when Trulliç didn't reply.

"Natural?" Marius asked, his head cocked to one side.

"Do you think that the desert magician isn't natural? That this isn't his true home?" Nadeem challenged.

"No, no. You misunderstand," Marius replied. "It is very obvious that all of this is his home. However, it is still part of the empire. He will need to pay tariffs and taxes, like everyone else."

Marius gave Trulliç a challenging look. Did he expect Trulliç to disagree?

"Of course," Trulliç replied. "I would welcome a visit from the emperor as well."

Trulliç didn't know if the soldiers believed him or not. He wasn't sure it mattered.

The emperor, or at least his representatives, had arrived.

Trulliç had to ensure they were well taken care of.

Or he would be facing the emperor, sooner rather than later.

"Are you ready?" Trulliç asked his new guests. The night was growing longer and he was already tired. Nadeem and Riyune still bolstered him, standing on either side. The guards formed a tight group before him. Quiet filled the desert, only the soft wind speaking.

"For what?" Marius asked.

"To go to Hayalevi," Trulliç said. He would have preferred to leave the guards there and make them walk the entire way to the city on their own. But he knew that would be rude. Seydat, as well as his mother, would yell at him for not treating his guests better.

Nadeem probably would have left them all without food or water, given the angry glares she shot their way. He wasn't sure if it was this group of guards or all of those in the emperor's employ that caused her to react like that.

Riyune, on the other hand, seemed resigned as only a dog could be.

"What do you mean?" Marius asked, confused.

"I will take you to Hayalevi with me," Trulliç told them.

"With magic?" Marius asked.

Trulliç paused. It appeared to be an important question to Marius.

"Yes," Trulliç replied. "Unless you want to walk all the way across the desert on your own?"

The men shifted, uneasy. The soldiers who carried swords put their hands on the hilts, while others gripped their pikes more tightly.

"We would like to see that," Marius said firmly, as if instructing his men.

"You are in for a treat," Nadeem said.

Trulliç glanced at her, curious. She gave him a quick smile. "Though it is unsettling at first," she added.

Trulliç reached out and gently touched all the men in front of him with desert winds. These weren't his people. He couldn't gather them in. Not like Nadeem and Riyune. They weren't desert creatures.

These men were foreigners, carrying foreign weapons. And he still couldn't figure out what made them so shifty, as if they did but didn't stand directly in front of him.

However, none of them had hidden away anything like the emperor's walking stick. Trulliç could ascertain the position of every man, where he stood, what he carried.

It wouldn't be difficult to disarm them. To cause all their weapons to fly away into the heart of the desert, for winds to scour their blades until nothing remained.

That would be rude as well. To remove all the support the guards relied on. What they felt protected them.

Trulliç wondered if they realized that the only thing that protected them once they stepped into his territory was his good will and the rules of hospitality.

With gentle winds, Trulliç lifted the group of guards, buffering them from the abrasive sands. He tried to make the start of their journey as placid as possible, so he didn't frighten the men.

They all wore stoic faces, determined not to show any emotions, though Trulliç smelled their fear, bitter and strong.

Only Marius appeared not to be afraid. He leaned forward, facing the winds. Though he also tried to keep his face grim, he couldn't help the smile that broke out now and again.

Trulliç kept their pace slow and even. They traveled much faster than any man or horse could have, but not as fast as a storm wind.

It would take them the rest of the night to arrive in Hayalevi. They'd arrive just after dawn.

Then there would be more questions. More awkwardness. More fencing with these "guests." What did they really want? And how much would the emperor demand for his tithe? Trulliç wasn't rich, and he was loathe to ask his people for money.

Hopefully Nadeem would help keep Trulliç from blowing the guards to pieces when they angered him, as they were sure to do.

In the meanwhile, he glanced over at her. She had her eyes closed, her arms and her head thrown back, as if she flew across the sky on unseen wings.

Riyune sat as still as a statue. The white of his fur glowed, making him seem ghostly.

Trulliç looked forward and let the happiness in his heart bubble up, filling himself with the sheer pleasure of the cool night and the unique feeling of having friends supporting him, all too aware that there was likely to be little joy in the coming days.

D awn had touched the great plain by the time Trulliç carried them to the edges of Hayalevi. The day promised brilliant warmth, the sky a searing blue.

Trulliç felt sorry for the guards, watching them wilt as the heat took hold. The sunlight invigorated him. He felt like a plant sometimes, just needing sunlight and water to live. Nadeem, too, looked refreshed, as if she'd just spent the night sleeping on a feather mattress instead of traveling across the desert and back.

Riyune gave him a great dog yawn and shook himself, but didn't leave after they touched down. Was he tired, too? Trulliç thought the dog's steps appeared to be dragging, but he couldn't tell for certain. He wouldn't be surprised, though, if Riyune slept through the heat of the day, as he generally did.

"Welcome to Hayalevi," Trulliç told the guards as they stood and stretched, shaking their heads. "If you'll come with me to my tower, I can give you refreshments and find you a place to rest for the day."

Marius nodded, stepping forward. "That would good," he said bluntly. Then he gave Trulliç a smile. "It was a magnificent flight. Magical. Thank you for that."

"You're welcome," Trulliç said, pleased.

The rest of the soldiers didn't appear to share Marius' wonder or enjoyment. They stamped the ground, obviously happy to be standing solidly on the earth again.

"Follow me," Trulliç said as the men gathered together.

"Did you, ah, raise, all of this?" Marius asked as they drew closer to the first buildings.

"I did," Trulliç affirmed.

He didn't like the greedy look that appeared in the soldier's eyes.

"Raising rocks and stones is easy," Trulliç continued. "But rocks and stones won't feed my people. Crops—trees—those are hard. I can't raise coins out of the ground." He'd learned a lot more about people's greed since he'd had to kill Gökel.

Marius nodded. He looked thoughtful.

Trulliç hoped that would put a dent in the soldier's appetite for taxes, though he doubted it would help much.

Was that why Atça had kept the buildings in Gaadiwala so poor looking? So the town wouldn't be so heavily taxed?

Trulliç didn't think that his former mentor would have considered that aspect of taking care of his people. As for Trulliç, it was too late now. He'd already started building his city. Plus, he wanted Hayalevi to appear as magnificent as it could. He intended to be proud of his city and its people.

"Tell me about raising the city," Marius said.

Trulliç told him about seeking water first, making sure to emphasize that he wasn't stealing water from anyone else. He talked of raising his tower, pointing out the glass that filled every window of every building they passed. Then he repeated Seydat's advice about creating the temples first, how they anchored the city.

"What building did you dedicate to the emperor?" Marius asked.

Trulliç didn't believe the man's innocent tone. "I haven't yet," he confessed, lying. "I was hoping that one of his representatives might help me plan something appropriate."

Marius seemed content with that response. However, he walked directly over to the next building they passed—a small square hut with an enclosed stone wall to keep the chickens in the yard. He peered intently at the base of it.

Trulliç knew who lived there—he knew everyone in his city. This small house belonged to a poorer couple who were childless. They'd had Trulliç create an altar to Innis inside the hut, taking up one entire wall, so they could pray to the god daily.

However, Trulliç didn't believe that Marius wanted an introduction to the people living inside. He dreaded having to ask, but knew that he must. "Is there something wrong?" he inquired when Marius continued to stay where he was and not make an effort to rejoin them.

"Where's the emperor's sign?" Marius asked. He pointed to the golden scale that covered his own red-leather chest plate. "All new structures should bear the sign of the emperor."

"Really?" Trulliç asked, acting surprised. "I didn't know that."

At the hard look Marius shot him, Trulliç merely shrugged. "Gaadiwala was such a small village and had so few new buildings."

Marius grudgingly nodded. "So you might not have known."

Trulliç turned, ready to keep walking, but Marius stayed stubbornly where he was.

"Yes?" Trulliç said. "Is there something else?"

"Can you add the mark now?" Marius asked directly.

Trulliç peered at the soldier. The question struck Trulliç as rude. However, he didn't think he could call the man out about his manners.

In addition, Marius seemed to already know the answer. He knew that Trulliç could shape anything in the buildings of his city.

"I can," Trulliç said. "But not now," he added when Marius appeared to be wanting him to do it immediately. "I've been awake all night and have expended a great deal of magic. I need to recover before I take on such an important task."

Marius pressed his lips together, as if biting back his words. Did he really want to challenge Trulliç on this? How much did the soldier know about magicians? How the land supported them, strengthened them? Marius wasn't magical himself. Trulliç would bet his own mother's life on that.

However, there was still something off about the man. Still something very different than with the other soldiers.

And Trulliç wasn't completely lying. He had expended a great deal of magic that night, flying to the edge of the desert, carrying them all back. Just before dawn he'd been quite tired.

Marius didn't need to know that it wasn't merely the land, but the sun itself, that strengthened Trulliç.

Finally, Marius seemed content to let it go. "Fine," he said as he walked away from the hut, rejoining his men. "But we should see to that first thing, placing the emperor's mark on all the buildings raised in Hayalevi."

Trulliç nodded, swallowing against a dry throat. He didn't want to mar the beautiful stone he'd raised.

He knew, however, that he didn't have a choice. Not if he wanted to maintain some semblance of peace between himself and the emperor.

Trulliç didn't know if he should be amused or horrified by his mother's reaction to the soldiers. She changed her demeanor from gracious desert host to tavern server in the blink of an eye. It wasn't that she treated their guests with disrespect. But her smile lost all its warmth, her tone became crisp and curt, and she held herself in such a way that she discouraged any familiarity.

The soldiers didn't know any better and so treated her with kindness, particularly when Trulliç introduced her as his mother.

The inside of the tower stayed cool even as the temperature outside rose. The men seemed grateful to be inside, out of the direct sun. Nadeem had left them there, claiming exhaustion, gladly taking up Seydat's offer of a place to stay. Riyune came and sat next to Trulliç like a regular dog, lolling on his side, resting his head on his paws and soon snoring.

Seydat and Myrizhah served them all sweet tea, flatbread, onions, and lard.

"Where do you get your salt?" Marius asked Trulliç, lifting the dish with salt and spices that were traditionally sprinkled on top of everything else.

Today Seydat had used a mixture of cumin, mint, and fennel with the salt. It had a sweet aftertaste that Trulliç liked, though as usual, he found himself eating out of habit and politeness, not because he was actually hungry.

Traditionally, salt came from towns along both coasts. However, Trulliç had no coastline to claim as his own. Mountains and foothills ringed the desert on all sides, not ocean.

"To the south," Trulliç grudgingly admitted. "There's a small salt flat." He'd been astonished to find it. At first he'd thought the sand was just colored white. It wasn't until he'd tasted it that he'd realized it was salt.

"Ah, very good," Marius said. "And the herbs?"

"From the fields just south of the city," Trulliç said.

"But we're in the desert!" Marius exclaimed.

Trulliç shrugged. Though the land to the south was much less arid than the rest of the desert, it was still *his*. "The mountains just beyond the fields provide some coolness. Rain flows over the tops and down the slopes."

"You'll have to take me there," Marius said.

While Marius' men were all too well trained to actually groan at the thought, Trulliç still could tell that they weren't enthusiastic about traveling more that day.

"Later," Marius added.

"Of course," Trulliç told him. "I'd be happy to take either just you, or you and some of your men."

Marius nodded. "What sort of caravans do you get through here?"

Trulliç found the question strange. "The city hasn't existed for much more than a month. We aren't on any regular caravan routes yet."

Marius' gave a look that showed how little he believed that. Maybe it was because the city had so many fine buildings that would have taken men many years to build.

Trulliç continued on. "Plus, it's the end of summer. Not many caravans are traveling this far south. Come spring, I expect to see quite a few." He hoped. He wanted his city to become a vital trading center, though he wasn't sure exactly how to achieve that.

"Maybe," Marius said slowly, his look of disbelief still firmly etched across his face.

Trulliç wondered how Marius was judging Hayalevi and if that just put another black mark against the city.

After the men had finished, Trulliç was the first to stand. "Come, let me make you a shelter where you can spend the rest of the day."

Marius stayed seated. "I think this is a fine place to stay," he drawled. "Don't you agree?" he asked the men.

Several nodded sleepily.

"Really, it wouldn't be a bother to build you all shelters," Trulliç said. He was desperate to get them to leave, to have his tower back to himself again.

"This place is fine," Marius said, his hard eyes belying his seemingly easy posture, how he stayed loose and leaned back.

Trulliç didn't know what to do. On the one hand, he needed to provide for his guests. That was his duty as a host. On the other hand, the guests shouldn't insist on staying in the house of the host if there was another place for them to go, if a suitable other location had been provided for them.

However, Trulliç didn't want to call the soldier out on his manners. Marius had been perfectly polite up until then. Trulliç tamped down on his own ready anger. While he could easily kill Marius and all his men, that wasn't the answer.

At least, not yet.

Myrizhah came into the room. She placed her hands on her hips and scowled at the men. "Shoo! All of you." She glared at Marius. "This is a place of business," she said primly. "All guests are greeted equally. Not made to squeeze in between you group of lollygaggers. Now go. Trulliç will provide you with adequate shelter."

Trulliç bit his lips together to prevent himself from grinning. He'd heard his mother use that exact same tone with patrons of the tavern who'd had too much beer or wine.

"Now, ma'am—" Marius started.

"Did you hear me, young man?" Myrizhah questioned, her voice like a whip.

Marius automatically sat up straighter.

Trulliç would bet that Marius' own mother sounded exactly like that when calling him to task.

"Yes, ma'am. I heard you," Marius said slowly.

"Then you will be on your way," Myrizhah said firmly. "Don't you want to watch the desert magician at his work? Calling forth the great stones from under the earth?"

"We do," Marius said, though he didn't stir. He wasn't beaten, not yet.

However, Myrizhah wasn't finished with him either.

"Then you will get up. Now. And accompany him," Myrizhah told him, her tone brooking no gainsay.

Marius at least was smart enough to know when he was beaten. "Fine, ma'am," he said, slowly rising. "We will leave your place of business."

Myrizhah merely sniffed at him, obviously disapproving of his slow capitulation.

Trulliç suspected that if the soldiers had done something equivalent in the Horseshoe Tavern, his mother would have cut them off, insisted on payment immediately, then kicked them out and not let them return.

The rest of the men complied, their displeasure apparent in every move.

Too bad. Myrizhah was right. This *was* a place of business, and they had no right to occupy it and disrupt what went on there.

"Thank you," Trulliç told his mother as the soldiers started to file out.

She peered at him, still upset, then sighed, her anger melting away. "You have a good heart, son," she said softly. "But I fear it will lead you astray."

Trulliç wasn't sure what she meant by that, but he wasn't about to ask. He'd never been that close to his mother. She'd always seemed so disappointed in him. She did appear to be prouder of him now, though he felt as if he hadn't gained her full approval.

Not yet.

Trulliç trudged out of the tower, following his guests. He knew that whatever building he raised for them would have to marked with the emperor's symbol.

He hated the idea of marring his beautiful stone with the emperor's mark. But he knew of no way around the decree.

Maybe he could talk with Nadeem, to get her to create illusions of the mark on the buildings, spells that would disappear when the soldiers left.

He doubted that would work. Marius, or one of the others, might be able to discern the difference.

Still, he decided to at least ask Nadeem about it.

Before he went ahead and just killed all the soldiers anyway.

Trulliç led the guards through the great market square (that was still mostly empty), past the temple to Innis, to an open area of land. To the north of them flowed the oasis trail river. Far to the south stood the fields.

After consulting with Marius, Trulliç built a three-walled structure for the soldiers, kind of like a large lean to, the kind normally built for goats or sheep. However, Marius insisted that was the structure he and his men were used to.

The long side of the building faced south, with a three-foot thick wall to keep out the worst of the sunlight. The east and west walls were also thick and solid, while the northern side was open, allowing in air and whatever breezes might stir. It could easily hold two dozen men.

The roof slanted from the open, high, northern wall down to the shorter, southern one. Marius insisted on plain dirt for the floor. Directly out from the northeast corner of the building, Trulliç raised a small well, using the smooth black stones that melted together like glass. On the opposite corner, he built an outhouse with a single bucket.

A line of long, thin windows ran across the tops of all the walls, just under the eaves. Trulliç covered them with a glass mesh: easily broken, but it would keep birds and bugs out, and allow breezes to come through.

Marius didn't seem impressed with anything that Trulliç did, though his men oohed and ahhed as the stones rose up out of the ground, forming themselves into bricks. Marius did seem to appreciate the well, particularly as it filled with water immediately.

But he looked dissatisfied when Trulliç finished.

Before the soldier could say anything, Trulliç asked, "Should I put the emperor's mark in the center of the roof? There?" He pointed to the open, northern edge. "That way everyone can see it."

Marius nodded slowly. "That would do."

Trulliç called up a piece of light-gray slate, fashioning it into a scale that looked exactly like the one on Marius' chest piece, then attached it to the building.

It looked like a turd on his beautiful work.

Marius appeared to appreciate it, however. "Nice," he said, nodding. Then he looked around. "How about a fence? Or a wall of some sort?"

Trulliç raised a short stone wall surrounding the area, giving the men a larger than normal yard, big enough for a dozen camels. With the wall came fig trees and a small garden of herbs.

It always surprised Trulliç when plants rose up with his stones. As if they, too, had just been sleeping under the ground, waiting for his call. He never felt them with the stones. They always came on their own. Still, he tried to act as if they'd been planned all along.

"Can you raise chickens as well?" Marius asked as he walked over to where the tiny lavender and rosemary bushes that grew beside the stone wall that enclosed the soldiers' building.

"Sorry—you'll have to buy your own," Trulliç said dryly.

Marius grunted as he brushed his fingertips across the tops of the plants. "Can you raise plants anywhere?" he asked. He seemed genuinely curious.

"No," Trulliç said. "There needs to be water. I've brought water to this place. And you're located close enough to the oasis trail for things to grow here. In the center of the dessert, where there's nothing but sand? I couldn't raise anything green or growing."

"But you could direct water there," Marius pointed out.

Trulliç shook his head. "Only if I stole it from someone else. And I would never do that."

Marius merely nodded, obviously thinking.

"I will meet you later this afternoon, then," Trulliç said, stepping back. "You need time to rest. As do I."

He didn't actually feel tired at all. The sunlight invigorated him. But he wasn't about to tell Marius that.

Marius opened his mouth as if to disagree, then thought the better of it. "Fine. This afternoon. Do you have a bell that rings the hours?"

"Not yet," Trulliç said. Bells were rung by the priests of Innis. Local people took care of the temples at this time. Hayalevi hadn't grown big enough to support priests.

"Then I will meet you here at two hand-spans," Marius said, turning and squinting toward the west.

It was the oldest way to tell time—by specifying the number of hands spans from the bottom edge of the sun to the horizon.

"I look forward to it," Trulliç lied as he hurried away.

He didn't know what Marius would insist on Trulliç doing when they met again.

He knew, however, that he wouldn't like it.

CHAPTER EIGHT

NADEEM

Nadeem gratefully took Seydat up on her offer of a quieter place to stay while the soldiers all gathered on the ground floor of Trulliç's tower. Though Trulliç could probably take care of himself if the soldiers offered any threat, Myrizhah would be the one to make sure they kept their manners.

After drinking a little sweet tea and eating some flatbread, Nadeem found herself surprisingly restless. She would have thought she'd be tired. She hadn't slept the previous night. The flight had been like a dream, with the golden, cool desert spread out beneath them and the black sky like an overstuffed quilt above. She'd caught the scent of musty desert mice, tantalizing traces of hidden springs, and the clear smell of dates somewhere in the far distance.

Nadeem found she couldn't sleep now. Not because she was afraid of her dreams, but something still niggled at her, bothered her, about the soldiers.

She sat up on the soft pallet that Seydat had given her, cleverly woven out of reeds from the oasis river, and listened. Seydat and Myrizhah still served the guards in the tower just next door. Seydat's two older children played in the yard behind the house. Chickens roosted there, giving quiet coos of contentment.

The room was very plain, the walls made out of the tall, thick stones that Trulliç built. Nadeem reached out and brushed her fingertips against the rock. It felt cool and dry, like the softest sand. The wound on her cheek gave a warning tingle, then went back to sleep.

Nadeem couldn't see any magic in the walls, though she was certain that a trace still remained. It didn't surprise her—this tower was Trulliç's heart, the epicenter of his power. Would the other buildings in Hayalevi give her the same feeling? Probably.

An open, glass-covered window stood far above the bed, with a matching one on the other side, so breezes might blow through the small room. Glass lamps hung from all four corners. The room was only as long as the bed, and maybe three times as wide, with a pounded dirt floor. A very nice braided rug lay in the center of it, colored brown and green.

Nadeem looked at her own hands and *blurred* the outline of them, making them indistinct. She knew that the eyes of anyone looking directly at her would slide off. Then she made herself darker. Though she didn't feel hollow, that appeared to be the effect. Just an outline of her hands and her arm remained. She looked like a shadow of herself. Against any dark background, she couldn't be seen.

No other star sister had this power, Nadeem was certain. Aunt Parayat hadn't proclaimed her an abomination, however.

Nadeem slipped out of her room, heading directly back to the tower. She arrived just as Marius announced that they would stay right there.

Nadeem had to bite her lips to hold back her giggles when Myrizhah rebuked him. Served him right. Who did he think he was, to disrupt their household that way?

It was obvious, though, that Marius expected for Trulliç and Myrizhah to meekly obey his wishes. She imagined that most of the citizens in the empire did just that.

The soldiers knew better than to try that sort of thing with the star sisters. Or perhaps the emperor had ordered them to pay the star sisters more respect, since some of them did special jobs for him.

Would the emperor send some of the special stars out after the desert heart? If so, how would Nadeem stop them? And then stop the next group the emperor sent? And the next?

The only way she knew to get the emperor to change his mind about acquiring the desert heart would be to destroy it before he could acquire it.

Or to kill the emperor.

But how? Now that the first group was here? How to stop them?

Nadeem had no doubt that Marius's true mission wasn't to see Trulliç but to find the desert heart. Hopefully Trulliç had figured that out as well.

Nadeem flitted from shadow to shadow, following Trulliç and the soldiers through Hayalevi, the market square, and finally, the place where Trulliç started to raise a great building for the soldiers to stay in. No one saw her. No one even looked in her direction, though she passed directly in front of more than one merchant calling out their wares.

She eagerly watched Trulliç start his new building. What a wonder—how the stones flew out of the earth and merged together. They changed color as they melded, the hues darkening into a brownish red. The smell of magic lay thick against the back of her throat, acrid and harsh like *igrat* that hadn't been allowed to age. Her cheek tingled, verging on painful, as magic winds caressed it.

It surprised Nadeem how ugly the mark of the emperor looked that Trulliç put on the building. It seemed completely out of place. Everything else Trulliç had raised or set his hand to had a grace and beauty to it. Why did this scale of the emperor's feel so different?

Nadeem stayed where she was after Trulliç hurried away from the soldiers. He didn't appear to notice her as he passed.

He could find her, she felt certain of that. Her magic didn't hide her from him. Only the emperor's stick had done that.

Instead, she drew closer to the soldiers, intending to spy on them. It was something she'd learned from Aunt Izmet, how important it was to learn about the enemy, study their strengths and weaknesses.

Plus, she was still certain that they were more than they seemed, and that they would immediately start searching for the desert heart.

However, the soldiers didn't appear to be doing anything out of the ordinary. They unpacked their packs, some settling in to sleep, while a couple began patrolling the stone wall set around their camp. Two others left, heading for the marketplace, coming back with chickens, bread, and some vegetables, obviously intending on starting their evening meal soon.

What was she missing? She couldn't see anything different about the soldiers. Couldn't determine their true nature. Didn't sense anything magical about them.

Patience had never been her strongest virtue. However, Nadeem settled down to wait in the shade. The soldiers would make a mistake and reveal themselves to her.

Then she could prepare.

———

Through the heat of the afternoon, the soldiers lazed around their camp. They didn't do *anything* that Nadeem found suspicious. Instead, a few started cooking their evening meal, others slept, while others sharpened and prepared their weapons, and a couple patrolled.

Nadeem remembered the hidden watcher of the Kardeş oasis. No one could hide here. The number of soldiers was too small, too easy to count. They weren't even behind four solid walls, merely a shelter of three, so everything they did could be seen.

More than one of the inhabitants of Hayalevi walked by the soldiers' encampment, obviously curious themselves. As far as Nadeem could tell, they didn't see anything out of the ordinary either. The people from the city stayed well away from the short stone wall that separated the soldiers from everyone else. Were they afraid of the emperor's soldiers?

After a couple of hours, Nadeem stood up from where she'd been sitting, stretching her legs. She wished for a moment that someone else could spell her, so she could walk around a bit. Sitting and waiting always wore at her.

"There you are," she heard someone quietly say from around the corner of the building. Someone obviously speaking directly to her.

Nadeem turned and walked that way, out of sight of the soldiers.

Trulliç stared at her, seeing her despite her shadows. "You've grown strong."

"Thank you," Nadeem said. She didn't see any point in denying it—her magic was much stronger than it had been.

"Like your aura, your magic has changed, hasn't it?" Trulliç asked, studying her. "You still cast illusions, but they're different, aren't they? It took me a while to find you, though once I figured out what I was looking for, it grew easier."

Nadeem merely nodded. She still wasn't about to tell Trulliç about rubbing the enchanted desert sand into her wound.

Trulliç glanced over to where the soldiers still did perfectly normal things. "I've been watching them too," he said. "But I can't tell what they're up to."

With a sigh, Nadeem admitted, "Me either. But they're here to find the desert heart," she added, warning him.

Trulliç stiffened for a moment, then he nodded. "That hadn't occurred to me. But I think you're right." He gave her a lopsided grin. "They aren't just here for me, are they?"

"They are not, young man," Nadeem said, using a prim auntie voice, teasing him.

Trulliç grinned at her. "So Mother told me as well."

"Your mother is wise," Nadeem said, meaning it.

Trulliç nodded, looking at the soldiers again. "I wanted to ask you about something." He paused, considering. "Is it possible to mark the buildings with an illusion of the emperor's mark? So that the soldiers are satisfied, but I don't have to permanently change the stone?"

Nadeem thought for a moment. It surprised her that he didn't want the emperor's mark on all of his buildings. Then again, given how ugly the one was on the soldier's encampment, maybe it wasn't that surprising after all. Did he hate the emperor that much?

"I could mark some of the buildings," she said slowly. "But I couldn't mark all of them. That's too many threads to keep track of." Her magic didn't permanently affect things. She couldn't cast an illusion and then walk away. She had to keep a tiny bit of her attention on any piece of magic she did if she wanted it to remain. While she'd been trained to track half a dozen small spells, much more than that and she'd lose track, so the illusions would disappear.

"That's what I thought," Trulliç said. He sighed.

"What is it?" Nadeem asked. Why did he not want the mark of the emperor in his town? Did he think himself separate from the emperor? Above him?

Should she have killed him as a traitor? Except she, herself, wasn't the most loyal to the emperor anymore either.

"I don't want him here," Trulliç whispered urgently. "I'm afraid that those marks will give him power over my city."

Nadeem's eyes widened. She hadn't considered that. "I don't know if that's how his magic works," she said slowly. Could the emperor reach out through his mark?

There was the legend of Lynds, who'd been able to reach all the star sisters through the mark they carried on their cheeks…

"Then what am I going to do? I know Marius will insist that I mark every building tonight," Trulliç said. His eyes grew colder. "I don't want to fight him, but I will."

Nadeem understood what Trulliç actually meant—that he'd kill the soldiers rather than give in to their demands. And that wouldn't be good for anyone.

"Is it possible for you to put a very shallow mark on the buildings? Something that would blow off in a day or so? I can follow along and make them seem as though they're more deeply set in the stone, at least at first," Nadeem volunteered.

"That would work," Trulliç said, nodding.

"Let's go try it," Nadeem said. She hadn't ever worked with a land magician before, trying to combine their magical skills. She suspected no star sister ever had.

Hopefully, it wouldn't be the last time they worked together. Because Nadeem really wanted there to be a song or story about them someday.

When the sun was two hand spans from the horizon, Trulliç presented himself at the soldiers' camp. Nadeem walked beside him, undisguised. Riyune kept pace as well.

Nadeem still wasn't sure what to make of the dog. He pretended to be an ordinary dog most of the time.

She'd seen him watching her with knowing eyes too many times, however. He reminded her of a blood hound, one of the dogs who shepherded pregnant women. She'd seen one in Kardeş when she'd gone to visit Aunt Parayat. But his coloring was all wrong, and Trulliç wasn't a pregnant girl.

At least as far as she could tell. She nearly giggled at the thought. Trulliç shot her a worried glance, but she merely smiled and kept it to herself.

The soldiers hadn't done anything other than what was expected of them for the rest of the afternoon: sleeping, guarding, preparing, cooking.

"Ah. Welcome, friends!" Marius said, greeting them both. He paused for a moment, looking curiously at Nadeem.

She raised her chin defiantly.

"I had thought you to be a star sister," Marius said. "Was I mistaken?"

Nadeem smiled coldly at him. "I am merely a traveler, now. I've given up my oaths."

"I see," Marius replied, his tone disapproving. "I've never heard of such a thing." He paused, then asked, "Does the sisterhood know?"

"I've seen and spoken with the aunt who raised me," Nadeem told him truthfully. "And she gave me her blessing."

Marius narrowed his eyes at her but didn't reply.

Trulliç spoke up. "Would you like a tour of Hayalevi now?"

Marius nodded, though he didn't stop staring at Nadeem. "Yes, please. We'd like to start with the temple dedicated to Innis."

Was that the temple that all the emperor's soldiers worshipped at? His symbol was a spear, and he was renown as a great warrior. She would have thought that they'd worship Barzhat, or Onnet, even.

But some of Marius's men did carry spears. It was as good of a place as any to start. And it was the temple closest to them.

Of course, not all of the men accompanied them. Only about half a dozen, with the rest of the two dozen staying behind, guarding the camp. Though Nadeem doubted that any of the people in Hayalevi would bother the soldiers. They didn't seem scared of them, not exactly. But she'd watched them all stare while at the same time never getting close enough to call out a greeting.

Would the streets ever be jammed with people? Nadeem didn't know. Trulliç had implied that at some point they would be. She couldn't see it.

Or maybe she couldn't see herself living in any crowd for too long.

Innis's temple had a spear fashioned out of black, smooth stone over the doorway. The temple was located in the southwest corner of the market square because Innis was also the god of good fortune and money, and tended to be the god favored by merchants and caravan owners. The dark stone of the building made it stand out from the red-gold that Trulliç generally favored.

Before they went inside, Trulliç made a great show of waving his hand over the cornerstone, carving the emperor's mark there. Nadeem silently made the mark appear as though it was carved deeply into the stone, instead of being barely scratched on the surface.

"Good," Marius said, approving when Trulliç finished. "The emperor will be well pleased."

Trulliç gave him a pleasant smile.

Nadeem hoped she was the only one who could smell the burning anger on him.

A few of the soldiers went inside to pray and make offerings. They chanted in beautiful, rich tones, singing a hymn Nadeem had never heard before about the fruitfulness of all things, the harvest, the hunt, and the home.

Next, they went to Onnet's temple, west of Innis's. Nadeem smiled when she realized it had been built horseshoe shaped. She and Trulliç went through the show of making the emperor's mark on the light-colored stone next to one of the benches set into the wall for the crones or for pregnant women to come and rest.

They visited the rest of the temples, the men making offerings, singing hymns, even dancing a few steps at both Enkat's temple as well as Barzhat's.

It was only as they were on the way back from Barzhat's temple that Marius stopped letting Trulliç lead. He turned and went back east another block or so. "What's that place?" he asked, pointing to a dark, cold building.

Nadeem shivered. She hadn't seen the small enclosure before. It was as though Trulliç had carved stones from the night sky and made a building.

Or from a nightmare.

How had Marius known about it? Nadeem would have sworn they hadn't passed it before.

"That's Forit's temple," Trulliç said slowly.

Marius stood, waiting.

Had Trulliç meant to skip it? The guard had specifically asked to tour all of the temples in Hayalevi.

How had he known about this one? It wasn't a usual temple. In fact, it was the first one Nadeem had ever even heard about.

Nadeem didn't like this temple. Why had Trulliç built it? The rocks felt out of place, as though carted in from some foreign land. They didn't have the smooth appearance of the rest of Trulliç's walls, instead looking like a giant with sharp fingernails had carved holes in the sides. No symbol of the goddess marked the outside walls.

What was Forit's symbol? Nadeem wasn't certain.

Marius stood next to the entrance of the temple, obviously waiting for Trulliç to set the emperor's mark in the cornerstone, as he had for the rest of the temples.

Trulliç glanced at Nadeem and shook his head. He didn't want her help with this one?

Nadeem kept her face smooth, not showing her confusion. She still stood beside Trulliç, just in case.

Winds swirled under Trulliç's direction, buffing smooth the cornerstone. He carved the same stylized snake's scale that he'd used on the other buildings. He stared hard at the stone, his hand extended, the muscles clenched as if he pressed against a solid wall. It was difficult to see the symbol, until Trulliç filled the outline with golden sand.

Marius just grunted. He didn't make any effort to enter the temple.

As Nadeem watched, the sand started spilling from the outline Trulliç had just carved.

After just a few moments, the wall reverted to its original pocked look.

"What is this?" Marius asked. He seemed more angry than puzzled.

Trulliç sighed. "This rock won't take any mark. Not mine, not the emperor's."

"Show me," Marius said. He appeared to be challenging Trulliç.

However, for once Trulliç didn't appear to react with anger. Instead, he shrugged, and put out his hand again.

Taller winds sprang up. Instead of merely touching the cornerstone of the temple, sand smoothed away a three foot high section. Into the center of it, Trulliç carved a curved shape.

Then Trulliç scooped up a handful of sand. He cupped his other hand over it.

Heat blasted out, making Nadeem take a step back. The white light that shot out from between Trulliç's cupped hands made her blink.

Trulliç pulled the light between his hands, as though it were taffy, then curved it.

Nadeem realized that he'd formed a horseshoe out of golden glass.

Trulliç floated the glass horseshoe through the air, pressing it into the carved mark on the wall.

It stayed there, shimmering for a few moments.

Then the glass darkened. Turned black. Dissolved into the wall as the mark disappeared.

Trulliç turned to Marius and shrugged. "The stones won't take anyone's mark," he said.

Marius grunted, staring at the wall.

Why did Trulliç raise this temple? Use these rocks?

Obviously, Nadeem was going to have to ask him about it later.

After a few more moments, Marius himself went into the temple. Trulliç and Nadeem followed him. The rest of the men stayed outside.

Were they scared? Or was it just because the temple wouldn't hold more than three or four comfortably?

Nadeem shivered in the cool air as she stepped across the threshold. Her cheek gave a warning tingle of pain, then subsided. One of Trulliç's glass lanterns burned in the corner inside the temple, hanging from the ceiling, suspended on an iron chain. It smelled of sweet incense, heavily spiced, though Nadeem didn't see any burning.

In fact, she didn't see an altar on the far wall. Just a gaping hole where the altar should be.

She looked questioningly at Trulliç. "This is the temple as it insisted on being built," he said defensively.

"I see," Marius said. He looked as though he'd just been handed a goblet of soured wine. "Just a placeholder? Not a proper place of worship?"

Trulliç shrugged. "The stones insisted on being built this way. I would have done more for the mother of us all."

Nadeem nodded. He was right. A temple to Forit should have been large and grand. When she'd fallen, her body had built the earth. Her blemishes had become all the people.

Yet, no one worshipped her, or built temples to her, even. Was it because she was a dead god and couldn't assist her followers? There were many hymns thanking Forit for her sacrifice, as well as holy days dedicated to her, but no temples or priests. She didn't demand anything from her followers, so she had none.

Marius crossed his arms over his chest and stared at the hole where the altar should be. Nadeem tried to see if there was any magic associated with that void, but she couldn't see anything special. If she had to guess, she'd say that the stones themselves held traces of magic. But she couldn't see what.

Marius finally nodded to himself, uncrossed his arms, and started singing a hymn of thanks to Forit. He had a surprisingly clear tenor, not the voice that Nadeem had expected.

Trulliç joined in after a few words. His voice blended well with Marius's, being a bit lower.

Hastily, Nadeem found her place and sang as well.

At the end of the hymn, Marius bowed his head, then turned and strode from the temple, as if he couldn't stand being in there any longer.

Trulliç followed quickly behind him.

Nadeem stayed for a few moments more. Their song echoed in her ears, as if the walls had clung to the noise and still reflected it.

Had the magic of the stone increased? Or decreased?

Nadeem shook her head, telling herself not to be fanciful. The walls were exactly the same as they had been when she'd walked into the temple.

Still, she was glad when she stepped outside again, into the warm air.

Trulliç and Marius discussed plans for an evening feast. They both acted as if nothing had happened.

Nadeem found her eyes being drawn back to the temple repeatedly.

There was something about that place. Something important.

Something that Marius knew and wasn't about to share with either of them.

***

Nadeem struggled to stay awake. It had been a long day preceded by no sleep the night before. She stifled her yawns and stayed focused on the temple of Forit. Watching the soldiers wouldn't tell her anything.

Somehow, Marius had known about this temple. Were there other soldiers that she'd missed? Or someone in town who worked with them? Maybe someone else who carried a cane, like the one she'd brought to Trulliç? Perhaps one of the merchants who'd passed information to them when they'd gone to the market for their dinner?

Trulliç had agreed to keep his attention focused on the soldiers and their encampment, while she stayed outside the temple.

Though the feast had lasted long into the night, Nadeem felt certain that the soldiers wouldn't stay and talk about taxes the next day, as Marius had promised.

Instead, they would seek out something at the temple. Do something.

Nadeem sat in the darkest of shadows next to the temple. No one could see her. The only way Trulliç would find her is through his magic, tracing her steps on the sand.

She wore tight black trousers and a black tunic, so she could move easily and fight. Instead of sandals, she wore mere strips of leather tied to her bare feet, again so she could run and fight. She had the traditional three knives of the star sisters tucked into her belt, along with blow darts and other weapons.

Trulliç had asked to watch her cast her illusions. Nadeem had nearly said no, but she'd let Levent watch when she'd left him. So she acquiesced, and let Trulliç watch her *blur* herself.

When she'd finished, Trulliç had merely smiled at her and said, "You are a marvel," before he'd walked away.

What had he meant by that?

Nadeem shook her head. She had to pay attention to what was in front of her. Nothing else.

The night air felt soft and cool around her. She heard the scuttling of mice and lizards taking advantage of the dark. Occasionally she heard the soft plunk of fish in the oasis trail river just past the temple. The smell of the heavy incense from inside the temple floated out to her now and again, though nothing sweet burned inside the temple itself. She assumed the scent came from the rocks themselves.

The night had mostly passed and the sky to the east began to have a slightly gray cast to it when Nadeem noticed movement.

Damn it! Had she fallen asleep?

No, that wasn't it. It was because mere shadows moved in front of her. Not men.

She blinked her eyes, making sure she understood what she was seeing.

The soldiers weren't as dark or as hollow as her. Her eyes didn't slide off their forms, as watchers did when she *blurred* herself.

They still weren't easy to see. She'd only noticed them because they'd moved. If they'd taken more time, creeping along, she might not have seen them at all.

Maybe because they hadn't been challenged all the way to the temple, they'd thought themselves safe.

Where was Trulliç? Had he been fooled? He must have been.

Nadeem waited until the three men had gone inside the temple before she moved herself. Quickly, she reached the door and peered inside.

The soldiers—Marius and two others—had already stripped off their disguises. They seemed weighted down with weapons, packs, and bags, as if they planned on being gone for a long time, crossing an inhospitable country.

Marius put his palms together and lowered his head, praying for a few moments. Nadeem realized with a start that he prayed to *the god emperor.*

She couldn't help her shiver.

It was so wrong for the emperor to want to raise himself up to the level of a god! She wasn't worried about the people rebelling from such a thing, but the gods' reaction.

She'd had so many dreams of the coming battles. Were they about to come true?

Marius's eyes glowed red when he finished his prayer and looked up.

Nadeem froze.

Marius was *not* magical on his own. He wasn't a magician. He certainly wasn't a star sister.

Instead, he appeared to be a conduit for someone else's magic. Able to channel magic from someone far away.

Nadeem would bet that the person's magic Marius channeled was the emperor's.

With glowing fingers, Marius reached up and tugged at his breastplate.

No, at the emperor's golden scale embossed on his armor.

Marius peeled the scale off his chest. A plain, merely painted scale lay underneath.

Using both hands, he pressed the scale against the far wall of the temple, that hole where the altar should be.

A sizzling noise filled the air. The foul scent of burning sulfur replaced the sweet scent of incense.

The dark hole widened. Lengthened. Until it was roughly man-shaped.

Beyond the opening, stars streamed. Nadeem nearly gasped when she realized it looked like the land outside of the small cavern that she'd rested in, the one that had rescued her after she'd mutilated the star sister mark on her cheek.

The men quickly marched through the gaping hole.

Nadeem hesitated. She had to go get Trulliç. Tell him what she'd seen. Though a part of her wanted to immediately go after the men.

She turned to run.

Before she got three steps more soldiers appeared out of the dark. They paid no attention to her, if they even saw her.

They ran as well, through the door of the temple. Out the back, to that other land.

Nadeem *raced* to the soldier's encampment.

No one remained there.

Trulliç sat against one of the buildings, fast asleep.

"Trulliç!" Nadeem said, kneeling next to him and shaking him.

Trulliç shook his head slowly. His mouth lolled, and his eyes didn't open.

Damn it! He'd been drugged.

When? During the feast, perhaps.

Nadeem had only pretended to drink the beer and wine that had been presented, as Aunt Izmet had taught her.

It hadn't occurred to her tell Trulliç not to have any. And Riyune lay fast asleep as well. Had he been drugged, too? Did the drugs that affected Trulliç affect his dog as well?

"Come on," Nadeem said, pinching Trulliç's cheek hard.

That at least got his eyes open. "The soldiers have all gone," Nadeem told him as he blinked groggily.

"Wha—" Trulliç said. He obviously was trying to fight off whatever they'd given him, shaking his head.

Deliberately, Trulliç placed one palm on the sand beside him and the other on Riyune's back.

Winds swirled up, creating small dust devils of sand.

Angry, heated winds carrying the smell of a dark storm pushed against Nadeem's back, making her cheek ache.

Trulliç blinked at Nadeem as the winds died down, sober. "Tell me what happened," he said plainly as he stood up. Riyune also stood, shaking his head, and then the rest of his body, hard enough that he nearly fell down.

Nadeem tugged on his hand. "Get us to Forit's temple first."

Trulliç nodded. He turned his own hand over so his burning hot, hard fingers intertwined with hers. They rose into the air and blew to the temple, racing faster than Nadeem had ever moved. It made her breath catch and her heart sing despite the dark deeds done that night, that they were about to go do.

As they stepped inside Forit's temple, the opening vanished.

Trulliç reached out with his hand. Could he reopen the portal?

He shook with the effort, but the stones resisted him.

The soldiers were gone, without a trace.

And they had no way to follow them.

Or to stop the emperor from bring death and destruction to them all.

CHAPTER NINE

TRULLIÇ

TRULLIÇ SHOOK HIS HEAD AND made Nadeem tell her story of the soldiers again. He couldn't feel them anywhere on the desert sands.

Trulliç stood with Nadeem outside Forit's temple, the dawn about to break. People were already up, the women baking bread in the cool of the morning, merchants preparing for their morning shoppers, roosters complaining loudly about the coming light.

"How could Marius channel magic?" Trulliç asked again. He didn't understand how the emperor had done that with the soldier. Was it a talent that all magicians had? Or was it something that only the emperor could do? Or was there something different about Marius?

Trulliç was viciously glad that he'd barely scratched the emperor's mark in all the buildings. He felt certain that his gut instinct had been right, that somehow the emperor could touch all of Hayalevi through those marks.

Trulliç would later go and destroy all of them, make sure his city remained apart from the Tanesh empire.

"I don't know how Marius channeled magic," Nadeem said, frustrated. "We have to go after them!"

"How?" Trulliç asked. "Where did they go?" The soldiers had obviously gone…somewhere. But where? He'd barely caught a glimpse of that other place before it had disappeared.

Nadeem paused, pressing her lips together. Trulliç waited. Finally, Nadeem said quietly, "I may know where they went. And how to get there."

"Really? Where? How?" Trulliç said, surprised. Creating magical doorways to other places didn't seem like star sister magic at all.

Nadeem took a deep breath before she answered. "There was a cavern that appeared out of nowhere. It was made out of rocks that looked like they were just piled on top of each other. Inside, there were shelves for sleeping and a small stream of clear water."

Trulliç held himself very still. It sounded like the place that he'd discovered on his first manhood journey. Or rather, the outcropping of rocks that had found him. "Go on," he said.

"I don't know how to get there," she said, shaking her head. "It just kind of appeared. I know, that sounds stupid. It had a guard stone just inside the door, like your tower does."

Trulliç nodded. It did sound as though they were talking about the same place.

"Beyond…beyond the door," Nadeem said, her voice falling to a whisper, "at night, the stars streamed across the sky. The soldiers went somewhere that looked the same. With the stars racing that way."

"Yes!" Trulliç said excitedly. "I've been to that cavern. It exists."

"Oh!" Nadeem said. "I was afraid I'd just dreamed it."

Trulliç nodded. "Me too," he said. "But I think it's real. There were gems—"

"Buried beneath it!" Nadeem said. "And if anyone dug for them—"

"The water would have been insulted and gone away, leaving them to die," Trulliç said.

"So it is real," Nadeem said, relieved. "But how do we get there? Or how do we call it?"

"I had the impression that it only came when one had great need," Trulliç said slowly.

Nadeem seemed thoughtful at that. But she nodded, agreeing.

What had been her great need? Had it been after she'd taken a knife to her cheek and removed the star sister's mark? Was that what had changed her magic? Going to that cavern? Or had it been something else?

"We need to call the cavern," she told him.

"You need to rest first," he told her.

"But—"

"The stars only streamed at night," Trulliç interrupted. "It does us no good to call the cavern now. We also need packs. And supplies."

"Fine. You're right," Nadeem said grudgingly. "But how are we going to call the cavern to us?"

Trulliç shrugged and said, "I am the desert magician." Hopefully the cavern would recognize him.

And their great need.

After Trulliç got Nadeem settled and resting, he went out again into Hayalevi, Riyune at his heels. He didn't need to rest, not like she did, not during the day. The sun energized him. Once the sun went down, he'd be tired. He'd try to nap later that afternoon.

For now, he had things to clean up.

More people were awake, merchants opening their windows or front doors so people could come in. Children screeched and raced along the street, playing a game of tag. A small herd of goats bleated as they meandered along, being herded toward the market place. The smells of fresh tea and cinnamon from someone's breakfast wafted through an open window.

The people of his city all had a smile and a "hello" for him, though no one tried to stop him and chat. He hoped that was because they could see he was busy, and not because they were afraid of him.

He went first to Forit's temple, but nothing there had changed. The black walls still felt cold, the sand on the floor undisturbed, as if no one had entered, the back wall blank and empty, a hole where the altar should be.

No foreign mark marred the walls on the outside either, where Trulliç had tried to place one earlier.

Pleased, he went to Barzhat's temple. Blue glass filled the windows, and a single line of black glass stood over the lintel, the symbol of the goddess. The temple was one of the few round places in the city, but that was how the stones had come out of the ground. Fine sand covered the floor, good for dancers and those who wanted to practice the steps they would give the goddess when they arrived at her golden court.

The mark of the emperor on the cornerstone was barely visible. Trulliç buffed the stone with sand and wind, clearing away the snake scale easily.

Trulliç breathed a huge sigh of relief. He'd been afraid that the rock would have been permanently infected by the mark, and that the emperor would already have a foothold in Trulliç's city.

Riyune seemed pleased as well, nodding at Trulliç as if he approved.

Trulliç visited the other temples in the reverse order that he'd traveled to them with the soldiers the day before. It filled him with satisfaction that he could easily clear the mark from all the cornerstones.

Last, he went to the building he'd raised for the soldiers. The large, pale-gray scale of the emperor's mark in the center of the roof appeared to catch the sun like a beacon. It made Trulliç shiver.

He'd never destroyed a building before. He wasn't sure where to start. Did he just sink the rocks beneath the ground? What about the fence and the plants there? Should he just leave the lean to, and tell the merchants they could have it for goats and other livestock?

Riyune leaned against Trulliç's leg. He had that feeling of acceptance again, that whatever he decided would be all right.

Trulliç peered more closely at the building. His ready anger came, fury at what the soldiers had done.

Not only did they trick him, they'd abused his hospitality. They'd drugged him at the feast he'd held in their honor.

He wrenched the gray stone scale from the roof of the building with some effort. He hadn't attached it that firmly. It felt to him as though the scale had grown roots and had started to infect the rest of the roof.

He sent stone flying high in the air above the city. If he could he would have sent it all the way to the emperor's court.

Instead, he focused his rage on it.

The stone exploded with a loud bang.

Trulliç called up winds to carry the dust and shards far into the foothills to the south, not wanting them to touch the interior of his city.

Then he reshaped the building. Made it smaller, less grand. Turned the well out front into an animal trough. Changed the latrine in the back into a compost heap. Opened the stone wall up, so it had many gates.

The earth greedily swallowed the remains of what the soldiers had left behind. After a few moments, no trace of them remained.

Trulliç found himself still breathing hard, his cheeks flaming, his blood pounding in his temples. How dare they? He coughed up his disgust and spat, unable to do more.

He wouldn't destroy a perfectly good building. The emperor and his soldiers couldn't make him that angry.

When he looked around, he realized that he had an audience. The people standing there gaped at him.

He could smell their fear.

Damn it! He kept doing the wrong thing. Soon, all his people would leave Hayalevi.

Riyune leaned against his leg again.

Trulliç's anger drained away.

His people weren't afraid of him.

They were worried about the emperor and what he would do next.

Trulliç stood on the top of his tower, the sun beating down on his head. He *breathed* in the desert air, smelling the baking sands and the far off salt flats. Winds stirred restlessly around him. He didn't see anyone in the streets below—everyone napped during the heat of the day.

Nadeem still slept as well. Trulliç envied her. Her dreams seemed sweet, not full of the anger and terror of his own. Riyune had stayed with her, laying down in front of her doorway as if guarding her.

Trulliç had one last thing to do before he also napped. Myrizhah and Seydat had already prepared their packs for them. Trulliç couldn't tell them how long they'd be gone, so the two women had spent the morning buying and baking travel rolls.

Water was their main concern. If the other side held true desert, Trulliç felt certain he could find water for them.

He had no idea what the other land held, though.

The emperor's stick floated in front of Trulliç, held by his winds. The silver snake's head glistened in the bright light.

The constant rage burning in Trulliç demanded that he sacrifice this thing. Break it into thousands of shards and hurl it far into the heart of the desert.

His hand shook as he fought to control his anger.

The emperor's symbol that he'd placed on the soldier's former building, yes, that deserved to be destroyed.

This walking stick, though, needed more care.

It still felt slippery to Trulliç. He had no other way to describe it. Whenever he tried to place it in his mind, to feel its place in his city as he could every stone and grain of sand, the stick slipped away, like a snake leaving its skin behind.

He didn't understand it. He didn't know what type of magic had made it.

And until he could learn more about it, he wouldn't just destroy it.

He knew they couldn't take the stick with them. Nadeem had told him how the cavern hadn't allowed the stick inside. But he also didn't want to just leave it here where it could do mischief.

He could, however, isolate it.

Trulliç loosened the glass horseshoe tied to his belt and held it in one hand. The stick remained floating in the air on his winds.

If Trulliç was being fanciful, he'd say that it felt to him as if the stick had just grown very still and wary, like a mouse hiding before a desert hawk.

More sand raised up in the air, swirling tightly around the floating cane. The acrid smell of magic flowed over Trulliç, chasing away the scent of the desert.

Light flashed from the silver snake's head, like a warning signal.

Trulliç's hand holding the glass horseshoe shook as he called forth more sand, more heat, more light. Angry storm winds howled around him. Lightning sizzled and crackled. The whirling sand grew as bright as the sun.

Trulliç refused to look away, letting the heat bake him dry of care and fear.

The stick stayed solid in itself, refusing to be transformed. Trulliç could break it. He couldn't change it.

Good thing that wasn't what he was trying.

With a soft *whump* the storm collapsed in on itself.

The winds trailed softly away.

Three inches of glass now encased the emperor's walking stick. It was primarily clear glass, with swirls of green and gold twirling through it, like Trulliç's horseshoe.

Now Trulliç felt the walking stick. Or rather, the glass around it. He could place it easily with his magical senses, not needing to rely on his sight to find it.

The stick remained exactly as it had been. But muted. No power trickled from it. No sense of its slippery nature. No light or magic.

Trulliç didn't think that the glass encasing the stick would hold it forever.

But for now, it would have to do.

Trulliç marched confidently over the sands. The sun hung barely a single hand span over the horizon. Riyune strode bravely beside him.

Or at least that was how Trulliç hoped he appeared. Or how people might sing of him, someday.

He was certain that Nadeem rolled her eyes at him behind his back. Riyune did frequently as well, though the dog hid his amusement less.

Trulliç had carried Riyune and Nadeem far into the heart of the desert itself. Sand spread all around them, as endless as the ocean that surrounded the Tanesh empire itself. Nothing stirred on the surface, though Trulliç knew that snakes, lizards, mice, and other small creatures lay resting in their hiding places, awaiting the cooler evening.

He wore his manhood tunic, the one that Myrizhah had bought him new for the first time he'd walked the desert. Under it, he wore a loose, unbleached shirt and baggy brown pants. His sandals were new, made out of solid leather and tied up the front, like the soldiers', instead of merely strapped to his ankle.

Food, a heavy travel roll, and as many skins of water as he could carry stuffed his pack. He figured Riyune could find his own food, as the dog frequently hunted mice and small animals.

He didn't bother carrying any weapon other than his eating knife. Nadeem had more than enough weapons for the pair of them. Possibly enough for a small troop of fighters.

She wore clothes that wouldn't necessarily be considered proper: tight black pants that didn't disguise the muscles in her legs, a black tunic belted just as tightly across her chest, and a sheer blouse. She wore knives on her belt, more knives strapped to her calves, her loose blouse sleeves hid darts, and her *chafiyek* held throwing stars.

Trulliç assumed she had more weapons hidden elsewhere. He didn't really want to know.

She also carried a pack full of food and water, almost as heavy as his own.

Trulliç wasn't sure how to call the desert cavern. He didn't think songs or praise would do it. The cavern knew its own worth, and wouldn't be swayed by flattery.

Could he convince it that his need was dire? Not his need for food or shelter, but for finding the soldiers? He wasn't certain.

Still, he strode up a slight dune, spread his legs wide in a solid stance, and sang out:

O sweetest water! What a welcome home!

He ignored how Riyune shook his head and rolled his eyes. Trulliç knew he had a good singing voice. He'd adapted a hymn for spring, welcoming the rains.

But the cavern didn't suddenly appear, even after he'd finished singing all three verses.

Nadeem merely nodded at him, as if congratulating him on his effort. "Can you feel the cavern anywhere?" she asked.

Trulliç closed his eyes and shoved his senses underground. Why hadn't he thought of that?

He pushed down on his anger. He couldn't think of everything. That was why he had help. No matter if her simple question had brought him back to the time when he doubted everything, when he was still a landless magician studying with Atça.

No water rested under the surface here. Only sand, rocks, and more rocks. No hidden sweet river.

He came back to himself and opened his eyes. "I don't feel it anywhere near here. Or anywhere out there, either," he added, gesturing to the desert around them.

"Ah," Nadeem said. She looked out at the horizon, then looked back at him. Her gaze felt heavy. "Songs won't work, I don't think. Nor dances, either."

Trulliç slowly nodded. She was probably right.

He was such a failure, destined to die here in the desert, his life bleeding away while the soldiers pillaged the desert heart.

"Try using blood to call the cavern here," she said.

"What?" Trulliç asked, blinking. Blood? What did she mean by that?

Nadeem drew out one of her knives—the one with the black blade. He felt a kinship to the knife. It was made out of obsidian.

"The cavern comes in times of great need," Nadeem said as she drew closer to him. She kept the blade in her right hand, while she held her left palm out toward him. "We are not dying. We have food. And water. But the world will die if we let don't stop the soldiers and the emperor claims the desert heart."

Trulliç nodded. She was right.

"I swear to do everything in my power, and beyond even that, given the help of the gods, to stop the emperor from laying waste to all the lands," Nadeem said. "This is my new oath. By my blood, I swear."

With a quick, clean cut, she sliced open her left palm. The blood welled up instantly. Nadeem made a fist, then shook her hand, once, twice, three times, scattering drops of red onto the golden sands.

Then she handed Trulliç the hilt of the knife.

He swallowed against a suddenly dry throat. He didn't want to actively go against the emperor. He still had hope that perhaps the emperor would just leave him be. Live and let live.

His mother would call him a foolish boy for such a hope.

Trulliç glanced over at Riyune, who watched with solemn eyes. He didn't seem inclined to take the same vow himself, but he also didn't seem to oppose Trulliç doing so.

With a shuddering breath, Trulliç took the knife and sliced open his palm.

The pain was a minor thing.

The heat of his blood mingling with Nadeem's took his breath away. What was she?

She cleared her throat, calling him back.

"By the full power of the desert, I swear to stop the emperor from desecrating this place, and the worlds beyond," Trulliç said, the words flying from him unheeded. "By my blood, I swear to pursue this, to the end of my days."

Like Nadeem, Trulliç made a fist to bring the blood more quickly to the surface. Then he shook his hand as well, scattering drops.

"There," Nadeem said when he looked up.

On the northern horizon stood a dark outcropping of rocks that hadn't been there just moments before.

"Our need is great," Trulliç told her as he handed back her knife.

Nadeem gave him a tight smile. "Let's hope our will is great enough to match it. Come on."

She took off toward the cavern, running down the slope of sand.

Was she whooping? Like a young girl?

He shook his head, then raced after her, letting joy fill his heart.

They were about to do desperate deeds.

It suddenly made more sense to find delight in the moments in between.

***

The cavern appeared the same as the first time Trulliç had seen it. The rocks felt as though they'd been haphazardly piled one on top of the next, then melted together. The tall stacks of rocks grew close together, like shoots of grass. Just inside the open doorway stood a guardian rock. He realized now that it was carved from different stone—granite, perhaps.

The outside of the cavern was roughly circular, but not exactly. More like someone's fis, laid on edge, with points sticking out. Long pieces of shale, roughly put together, covered the roof.

Both Trulliç and Nadeem walked all the way around the cavern before stepping inside. The air just beyond the guard stone felt cooler and softer. Trulliç immediately set his mage light glowing in the center of the room so they could see.

Trulliç couldn't help but smile at the soft trickle of water that he heard. He would have to ask Nadeem, but they might empty out all their water skins and refill them with the water from the cavern, even if there wasn't anything magical about it.

Nadeem already knelt next to the stream, bathing her cut hand. "Here." She directed him to do the same.

Trulliç shivered as the lukewarm water caressed his skin, the stream tasting his blood.

"We are still sworn," Nadeem whispered. She appeared to be talking to the stream.

After another moment, she stood, stretching, then took off her pack. "We'll be here for a while, until it's fully night," she told him.

Trulliç nodded, drawing his hand out of the water. The line across his palm had already closed up. Just a thin white scar showed.

Nadeem asked, "Was this your first blood oath?"

"Yes," Trulliç said. "I've never had to take one before. But it wasn't your first blood oath, was it?"

Nadeem laughed softly. "No. Far from it. I had thought the oath to kill you would have been the last one I took. But I was wrong." She stretched out on one of the upper shelves, relaxing.

Trulliç dropped his eyes back to the water. Nadeem was very… distracting, dressed as she was, now wiggling and making herself comfortable that way.

"What was your great need?" Nadeem asked after a few moments. "That brought you into the cavern the first time?"

Trulliç stood. Now that Nadeem appeared to be settled, he could settle in himself. He stepped over the stream and lay down on the very bottom shelf, stretching out.

He told her about his manhood journey and walking the desert the first time. About Atça drugging his water with *agafi*, not realizing (or not caring) that it would make him feel so restless.

"I met Riyune here, too," Trulliç added. He turned his head, looking over at the dog who lay on the far side of the small stream, looking as ordinary as he ever did. "He first appeared as a blood hound. Though that might have been a dream."

He heard shifting above him, as if Nadeem, too, had turned to look at the dog. "He has the same shadow as a blood hound," she said softly.

Riyune lifted his head, growing as still as a statue. He stared hard at the pair of them, as if judging the best way to rip out their throats.

Careful! Trulliç wanted to cry out.

But Nadeem just laughed. "Made me wonder if you were pregnant or something," she said lightly.

Trulliç heard Nadeem shift again, rolling onto her back.

"Wake me when the star show starts," she said sleepily.

Trulliç knew that in moments, Nadeem would be asleep. It must have been part of her training, to sleep wherever and whenever she had the chance.

He sighed and looked back at Riyune, who'd gone back to being an ordinary dog.

What was Riyune, exactly? Who was he?

Coming back to the place where Trulliç had first met the dog just raised more questions, not answers.

Trulliç dreamed.

He knew he wasn't awake because his mage light had changed from yellow to a deep purple, casting long shadows through the cavern. From where he lay on the bottom shelf, he could barely see around the guard stone. In the dream, the guard stone still stood, but it had grown transparent, just a gray mesh that he could see through.

Riyune had stayed on the far side of the stream before Trulliç had gone to sleep. Now the dog rose, shook itself and went to stand in the doorway.

A thin howl filled the air.

Trulliç *had* to be dreaming. Riyune never barked. He certainly didn't howl.

At least half a dozen figures floated across the sands.

In that way of dreams, Trulliç knew that these were the ghosts of the dead kings, those who had once ruled Osmerli, the city that had stood in the desert before Hayalevi. They had tall crowns that had grown jagged and sharp, like brittle stone. Their eyes shone black in their white faces. Long silver hair made up their beards.

They looked as gaunt as starving men. The closest reached out to touch Riyune's head with skeletal fingers, blessing him.

Trulliç couldn't hear what the old kings said. Their counsel for Riyune came to him as hisses and swishing wind. They carried the smell of old incense, weak and sour. He tried to raise his hand, to ask them what they wanted, but sleep had shackled his wrists to the rock he lay on.

The guard stone grew more solid as Riyune stepped back around it.

The dog dropped beside the stream, collapsing into sleep, his gentle snores filling the small space as if he'd never left it.

Trulliç sighed. He'd wished he could have talked with the old kings. See if they had any advice for how to fight the emperor. But maybe his next dream would bring him to them.

He let sleep carry him away again.

* * *

A soft *plop* woke Trulliç. He started, the sound out of place.

Nadeem had already leaped down from her shelf, knife in her hand. She stood and stretched, laughing.

"Riyune thinks we've slept long enough," she told Trulliç over her shoulder.

Trulliç looked past Nadeem to the dog who tried to look innocent and not as though he had a couple more rocks ready to cast into the stream in order to wake them.

Nadeem grabbed her pack and walked to the opening of the cavern. She gave a low whistle.

"What?" Trulliç said. He got up and went to the opening, peering out beside her.

Stars streamed across the black sky. Golden sands spread out before him, like a soft carpet. The smell of salt and smoke floated by, carried on a wind, here and gone.

Nadeem quickly tied all her weapons to her, then slipped on her pack. "I'm going scouting," she told him. "If I'm not back in an hour or so, see if you can make it back."

"But—" Trulliç said.

"If I can't make it, you probably won't be able to either," Nadeem told him firmly.

Trulliç sighed. She might be right. "Safe trails and easy water," he told her. It was one of the traditional farewells that people gave each other.

She gave him a brilliant smile. "Good winds and easy water," she told him. Then she slipped out of the cavern onto the shining sands.

Trulliç knew that his mage light hadn't wavered. The cavern was just as brightly lit as it had been a moment before.

It still seemed dimmer, the shadows darker, without her there.

Riyune sat beside Trulliç as they watched Nadeem walk away from the cavern. The dog looked up at Trulliç expectantly.

"She told me to wait," Trulliç explained.

Riyune seemed to be wanting more.

"So we wait. At least a little while," Trulliç added.

Riyune looked at Trulliç, then back out, over the sands. He looked as though he would chase after Nadeem in a heartbeat if only Trulliç would give the word.

Trulliç made himself wait. Watch.

The figure on the sands grew smaller.

Abruptly, Nadeem disappeared.

Trulliç surged to his feet. He swallowed against a dry throat. "She said to wait…" he said.

He looked again at Riyune.

Though the dog didn't say anything, didn't actually speak words, his look certain spoke volumes.

Go after her. Idiot.

"You're right," Trulliç said. He slipped on his pack.

Paused.

Turned back toward the center of the cavern. "Thank you for your hospitality," he said plainly. "For the wonderful fresh water and safe bed."

He didn't know if the cavern heard him, if the stream understood, but he would be a poor guest if he didn't thank his host.

Then he slipped out of the cavern, onto unknown sands.

CHAPTER TEN

NADEEM

THIS PLACE WAS, BUT WASN'T, the same as the desert in Nadeem's visions, the ones she'd had since she was little, before her initiation ceremony, even.

The ground remained soft glittering sand beneath her feet. She still feared it would turn to crunchy ash, filled with the tiny shards of burned bones. The sky streamed with stars, lights leading her path. Gentle winds tickled the back of her neck, carrying the smell of briny water. The sand, too, flowed along.

Loneliness filled her. Even at the heart of the desert, where few animals or insects lived, she still felt part of *something*.

This place was isolated. Nothing lived here. Not even the tiniest of biting flies.

It didn't surprise Nadeem when she turned back that the cavern had disappeared. Nothing living remained on this landscape.

Nothing but her.

There was no way back to her home. Her desert. Her old life or her sisters.

Trulliç would have to find his own way. Just as she would.

Nadeem turned forward again, willing to follow the stars.

Nadeem pushed herself to run, forcing one foot in front of the other. The sand fought her, making her sink down. Sticking to her feet, gritty against her skin.

Though the air stayed calm, it felt as though she battled great winds, full of the sour smell of her own sweat.

She struggled, trying to glide as she had in the Qaenev desert. While she couldn't go as fast as Trulliç, surely she should be able to run here.

The land accepted only walking, however.

Panting, Nadeem slowed and started moving at a slower pace. Her steps became easy again.

Though this was a desert and it was related to the Qaenev, it wasn't the same. She didn't have the same power here.

Trulliç probably wouldn't have the same amount of magic here either.

Nadeem had no idea how long she'd been walking. The stars streamed over her head—she couldn't tell if it was still the middle of the night or close to dawn. She smelled briny water on the winds, so she knew she could refill her water skins.

So she couldn't run. Nadeem stopped and turned around, looking back at the way she'd come.

Even just standing still bothered this place. It wanted her to keep going. Everything *flowed* in a single direction—the sand, the stars, the winds. She was only supposed to go one way.

Stubbornly, Nadeem tried to retrace her steps. She found herself sweating in the cool night air, her legs trembling with the effort, cursing like her old teammate Duzhen. It made her smile until she realized just how alone she was again.

Reluctantly, Nadeem turned and went the easier direction. The land was too big to fight on her own.

Suddenly, a white blur raced past her.

Nadeem stopped, reaching automatically for one of the knives at her belt.

Riyune sat in front of her. He glared at her, daring her to try to harm him.

Nadeem replaced the knife slowly. She remembered Riyune at the cavern, when he'd grown fierce and still, a predator debating whether to kill his prey now or later.

She didn't trust this dog. If he was a dog. He appeared skeletal in this land, more like fur-covered bones than flesh and blood.

But if Riyune was here…Nadeem turned.

Trulliç walked briskly across the sand. He wasn't floating like he usually did.

Nadeem scolded herself for her small heart that he couldn't move that quickly here either.

"How did you get so far?" Trulliç asked. He seemed angrier than usual. "Why did you disappear?"

"I didn't," Nadeem said. She felt her own anger brewing. "I just walked. Following the desert."

"Oh," Trulliç said, deflating. "I thought…I thought you'd just left. Abandoned me."

"Why would I do that?" Nadeem asked, truly puzzled. "You're the desert magician. We're in a desert. It isn't the Qaenev, but surely you have some power here. Why would I throw that away?"

If the light had been better, Nadeem would have bet that Trulliç blushed.

"I thought…I just thought—"

"You just let Atça back into your head," Nadeem told him.

Trulliç looked down at the ground, ashamed.

"Look, I've already had to point out to you that you were the desert magician," Nadeem said. "Don't make me have to beat some sense into you this time."

"You sound like my mother," Trulliç said. He sounded horrified.

"Your mother is a wise woman," Nadeem told him seriously.

"She is," Trulliç said. He paused, then added, "She thinks I have a good heart. But she's worried that it isn't enough."

Nadeem firmly kept her lips pressed together so she wouldn't say anything.

From the look Trulliç gave her, she knew he heard the words anyway. That she, too, was worried that his good heart wouldn't be enough at the end.

Dawn came all at once in this strange land. Stars streamed in a midnight sky until all of a sudden, the sky lightened. It was as if someone had lit a lamp, causing the sky to brighten.

Nadeem shivered in the abrupt heat. It unnerved her, how quickly the night had passed.

It also meant that later, night would leap upon them without warning.

Trulliç seemed just as unsettled walking beside her, but he didn't say anything. They just kept going. Riyune kept pace with them, moving in a strangely direct manner. Normally, dogs would go off chasing scents, straying in front of them then trailing behind.

But Riyune seemed just as determined to get where they were going without additional forays.

The horizon changed abruptly, as if they'd just climbed a hill and could now see off into the distance. Instead of clear blue, the sky grew gray and dark.

Nadeem feared what was coming next.

"Doesn't smell like a storm," Trulliç told her, pausing.

"I've dreamed of this place," Nadeem quietly admitted.

Trulliç raised an eyebrow at her.

"It's where the end of the world occurs," she told him.

He nodded. "It feels like the end of the earth, doesn't it? As if nothing lays just beyond those clouds."

"So lonely," Nadeem said.

Trulliç cleared his throat, as if he was about to argue. Then he shook his head. "Let's make sure it isn't the end," he said firmly.

They started walking again, into the great unknown.

The sand changed as Nadeem feared it would, covered in ash and tiny bones that cracked as she walked. She was glad she had on proper sandals and not just strips of leather tied to her feet.

Trulliç grimaced as he walked. He tried to lift himself up, but the effort to do so wasn't worth it.

The land wore at Nadeem's soul. To the right lay a great wooden wall, tall as a two-story house. It curved both at the top and the bottom, though, as if it weren't a solid block, but a rounded piece.

Like the handle of a great spear.

"We're getting closer," Nadeem told Trulliç. She wanted to run. To race toward that death she knew was waiting for her, fighting an endless stream of gibbering darkness. To go and dance in the goddess's court before the rest of the world did, before it all came crashing down.

She also wanted to drag her feet. To delay the end and keep breathing the sweet desert air as long as possible.

Trulliç put up his hands in front of him. "I'm trying to see if I can feel anything different," he explained to her. "All I feel is death."

Nadeem nodded. As a star sister, she'd agreed to love Barzhat, the goddess of death. She'd invited the goddess to all of her meals, welcomed her into her heart.

This place should have felt like home, in a way. But it was the farthest thing from it that Nadeem could imagine.

Riyune stopped abruptly, causing Nadeem and Trulliç to pause as well.

Figures moved on the far horizon. They resolved into a group of men, maybe a dozen in all.

"The soldiers," Nadeem said.

"Aye," Trulliç replied. He looked over at Nadeem. "Do you think you could hide?" he asked.

"I can try," she said. She stared at her hands, willing them to *blur*.

Slowly, oh so slowly, the outline of her skin changed. She felt as though she fought the very air to make the illusion work. Her cheek ached, pain beating in time with her heart. Sweat broke out along her back and slid down her hair, under her *chafiyek*.

"Don't," Trulliç told her after a few moments.

Stubbornly, Nadeem kept trying to complete the effect, to be not only blurred but hollow.

"Don't waste your strength that way," Trulliç said after a few more moments.

Panting, Nadeem lowered her hands. Trulliç was right. The land wanted her as she was, not changed.

Maybe that would give them an advantage, though. If she couldn't change, maybe Marius couldn't either.

"Can you do any magic here?" Nadeem asked Trulliç.

He shrugged. "Some. I can find water. I can raise rocks. And I can create glass," he said. "But all at great effort."

"Let's hope it's enough," Nadeem said.

In the end, it wouldn't be Trulliç or his heart that would be tested. It would be hers.

———

The soldiers stood in four solid lines, facing them as they approached. The foul smell of rotting blood filled the air. Dark clouds stretched over them, unnatural, a storm that would never bring rain.

Nadeem's breath caught when she realized that a small outcropping of rock stood behind the soldiers. It looked the twin of the cavern she and Trulliç had called to get to this place.

She's seen something like it before in her visions. Once it had held back the darkness brewing inside with a thin red string.

Here, a great gray guard stone stood just outside the entrance, blocking the way.

Whatever was inside the cavern sickened Nadeem, making her stomach knot and clench.

Marius stood in front of the guard stone. He'd drawn the emperor's mark in black charcoal on the gray stone. He paid no attention to his visitors. He held his hands out, obviously trying to channel magic through them onto the large mark.

He shook with the effort. Acrid magic swirled around him. A dingy layer of fog undulated at his feet.

However, he didn't appear to be very successful. The stone in front of him resisted his efforts to break it.

Nadeem was shocked at Marius's appearance. He seemed hollow, as if all the efforts he'd made here had started eating at him from the inside out. His cheekbones stood out on his face, and his skin hung loosely from his skull, as if he'd lost a great deal of weight. His eyes burned black with rage. The muscles on his arms had shrunk, and wrinkles covered all his skin, as if he'd turned into an old man overnight.

"Grab them," he ordered his soldiers.

Nadeem laughed. She pushed Trulliç behind her and easily took out the first three soldiers. Did they know nothing about the star sisters?

She didn't expect Trulliç to be able to fight, but a great wind howled past her, knocking over another two soldiers.

Even Riyune joined in, harrying one of the bow bearers, tearing the skin and muscle just above his mid-calf sandals.

Nadeem laughed again as she spun, slicing skin as easily as she did air. She felt as though Barzhat had come to visit, lending Nadeem the goddess's strength and grace. She moved as easily as her hawk girl did when she'd been fighting illusionary battles with her sisters.

Pivot. Slice. Block. Duck. Kick. Kill.

Was this the dance that the goddess would demand from Nadeem when she entered her court? Nadeem had never killed before, but these men didn't seem real, despite the fact that their blood now coated her hands, her nose was full of the stench of their spilled bile, her ears still rang with their angry cries.

"No! Stop!" Trulliç called.

She glanced back at him. He stood alone. No one threatened him.

She turned back to the soldier standing in front of her and speared him with her knife, stabbing his neck and driving her blade to the hilt into his skin.

When she stepped back, he dropped slowly, collapsing like a falling leaf.

Trulliç came rushing up to her. He seemed really angry. "What?" she asked defensively. She'd just saved their lives. Hadn't she?

He merely pointed toward the outcropping of rock.

Marius hadn't joined the fight. He'd gone back to where they'd first seen him, hands extended, trying to magically blast through the guard stone.

Only this time, the magic was working.

Nadeem swallowed down her bile when she realized that Marius was *using* the deaths of his soldiers to power his magic.

Black clouds rose from the fallen men, wafting toward Marius, making his mage light stronger.

Who used the dead to make themselves stronger? Nadeem had never heard of that type of magician before.

Then she shivered, realizing that *this* was the power of the emperor. This was why the kingdom of Tanesh had constant wars.

The emperor needed to feed off them.

By loosening the desert heart and that gibbering blackness on the world, the emperor would become the strongest being on earth.

He would become a god. Possibly, the only one remaining.

Trulliç called up mighty winds, trying to disrupt the flow of power from the dead soldiers to Marius, but the magical draw was too strong. A physical wind couldn't stop the energy Marius drew from the soldiers.

Riyune raced around, looking possessed, leaping up in the air and trying to bite the black clouds. His mouth grew bloody, as if he was biting glass.

Nadeem couldn't see any way to disturb the streams of magic flowing to Marius. The emperor's mark in the guard stone glowed with a sickly yellow.

All she could do would be to stop him.

She drew her first knife and threw it directly at the center of Marius's unprotected neck. The armor dipped there, probably to help cool the soldiers off.

Barzhat still guided her hand.

The knife sunk into Marius's skin. He gave a terrified wail as he dropped down. The magic he'd been channeling blew him to pieces with a loud splat.

Nadeem hurried over to where Marius had been standing, avoiding the large gory mess that covered the ground.

The guard stone still stood. But it trembled mightily.

The heart of the rock had been cut out. Darkness loomed just on the other side.

It was only a matter of time before it broke and the world was consumed by nightmares.

Nadeem dropped another rock in front of the cavern door. She and Trulliç attempted to reinforce the guard stone.

Their pitifully small pile of rocks wouldn't impede anything, however. This place didn't accept *change*. It wouldn't have surprised Nadeem if after another night of streaming stars, all the grudging rocks that they'd moved would have gone back to their original places.

Trulliç couldn't raise another guard stone in front of the one standing.

No rocks could be called out of the ash here. He called rocks from the desert that surrounded them, but they came unwillingly into this place.

They had to do something. Cracks now ran from top to bottom of the guard stone. Something on the inside of the cavern wanted out.

Now.

"I don't think this is working," Nadeem told Trulliç as he struggled to lift a great boulder with his magic.

He sighed, dropping the stone to the ground with a soft *whump*. "I agree," he said. "Do you have any other ideas?"

Nadeem looked at him. Then back at the guard stone. "You said you'd enclosed the emperor's walking stick in glass," she said slowly.

Trulliç nodded. "I'm not sure how long it will last. That stick is… slippery. But it will hold for a while."

"You could try encasing the guard stone in glass," Nadeem said.

"That might work!" Trulliç said excitedly. "I'll start with a thinner coating of glass, then build it up."

Even if that didn't work long term, it would at least give them some time before darkness fell and the stone broke.

Trulliç stood before the door. Nadeem shivered when she realized that he'd adopted the same stance as Marius had.

Ash and sand swirled up, dancing in front of the stone. It wouldn't be a clear glass, she knew.

After a moment, the sand fell back. Trulliç stood, panting, as if he'd just run a mile or more.

"Let me try again," he said. This time, held his glass horseshoe in one hand, pointing the ends of it at the guard stone.

The sands and ash swirled up again. Heat also blasted forth.

"Careful!" Nadeem warned. She didn't want him to break the guard stone with his magic.

Trulliç merely grunted. The heat didn't lessen. However, he did take a step backwards, bringing the heat with him.

Light sprang up, bright enough to make Nadeem's eyes start watering. She blinked, looked away, then forced herself to keep watching, even if it was out of the corner of her eye.

A great glass wall formed. Swirls of ash ran through it, like long lines of dripping mud.

Nadeem caught her breath. Would it hold?

Slowly, the glass encased the guard stone. It was easily as thick as her arm, obscuring the gray stone behind it.

When Trulliç stepped back, Nadeem drew a breath of relief. The stone would hold.

A booming *crack* rang out.

The glass shattered, falling to pieces at the foot of the guard stone.

The rock bulged ominously.

They were running out of time.

"How did Forit bind the darkness?" Nadeem asked Trulliç as they stood in front of the ruins of their attempts.

The bodies behind them stank, putrefying in the dim light. Night would fall soon.

And so would the rest of the world.

"She sang such a sweet song that she coaxed the darkness to expose its heart," Trulliç replied, as if reciting a lesson. "But the only way to entice the heart of the darkness was to use her own. Innis didn't realize that he was killing his wife when he stabbed the darkness."

Nadeem nodded. "Sacrifice," she said solemnly.

That was what a blood oath really represented. The sacrifice one was willing to make.

"Blood and death broke the guard stone," Nadeem announced, standing up and walking closer to it. "Only blood and death will heal it."

Trulliç looked pale under his tanned skin. "Yours?" he asked. His voice squeaked.

"You need to go back and fight the emperor," Nadeem told him firmly. "I can't do that. I can only stop him, here." As she had sworn to do. He would never get through the guard of her heart.

"I can't," Trulliç said. He rose finally and came over to her. "I just… Why?" He trembled where he stood, looking as though a strong wind would knock him over.

Nadeem took out her sacrificial knife, the one that she's used to swear a blood oath to Trulliç. "If you don't do it, I'll do it myself," she promised him.

This close to the guard stone, she felt the darkness clawing at her back. It welcomed her death and wanted to consume her.

She could not allow that to happen.

She would stand guard here instead, until the end of days.

"The only way to keep the guard stone alive is to renew it," she said. She sounded more sure of herself than she felt. "It needs another sacrifice."

Trulliç swallowed, still bothered. "Can't it be someone else?" he whispered.

She looked into his haunted eyes. Trulliç had killed before. Hell, he'd even twisted the necks of more than one of the soldiers with his winds, ending their days.

"You have a good heart," Nadeem said deliberately.

Trulliç flinched.

"Now you must be strong enough to do what needs to be done," she said. She held the knife out to him, pleased that her own hand didn't shake.

"No," Trulliç whispered. He stared at the knife in horror.

When he looked up, tears streamed down his face. "Don't make me do this."

"Then I will do it myself," Nadeem said, reaching for the blade.

Trulliç snatched his hand away surprisingly fast. "I don't want to sacrifice you," he said, looking away, as if afraid to show her too much by looking at her.

"It's the only way to save the world," Nadeem assured him.

She knew she was right. Felt it like the goddess's embrace, deep in her bones. There was no going back for her. Only forward, into the sands.

She wrapped both her hands around his, the one holding the knife. Then she brought the blade forward so it kissed her breast.

"It's sharp enough to go straight in," she told him. "It won't take much effort at all."

Trulliç gave her a crooked grin. "That's what you think," he said. His eyes bored into hers. He cared for her. More than she'd realized.

More than they could ever explore.

"I'll say hello to the goddess for you," Nadeem said. "Make sure your own weights aren't too heavy."

The stone behind her gave a resounding crack.

"Now!" Nadeem ordered Trulliç. She tried to force his hand holding the knife closer, the tip of the blade breaking her skin.

"No!" Trulliç wailed. He began to press the blade in.

A white whirl snatched Trulliç's hand away.

Riyune held the blade in his mouth.

Then he tossed it into the air, like he frequently tossed mice up, by their tails, to swallow them whole for his dinner.

Only the blade struck his open mouth, ramming down the back of his throat, the tip shoving its way through the fur of his neck.

Nadeem shook, horrified.

Why had Riyune sacrificed himself that way?

She felt bad that her next thought was: Would it work?

Trulliç raced over and knelt down next to his fallen companion. Tears streamed down his face. "Why?" he asked, sounding heartbroken.

Nadeem shook her head. She didn't know.

The dog was already dead by the time she drew closer.

The guard stone shook. The foul scent of darkness wafted out, smelling like rotting reeds and long forgotten pain.

Nadeem helped Trulliç lift Riyune's lifeless body. The knife fell to the ground with a startling clang as it hit the rocks.

Nadeem let it lay where it fell.

They carried the dog's body to the guard stone, lifting it up, placing it over where Marius had carved the emperor's mark.

As they pressed Riyune against the rock, his body dissolved *into* the stone.

Nadeem kept pushing. She felt like a baker, kneading a stiff dough, trying to force it into an unfamiliar shape.

When they stepped back, the guard stone stood firm. Trickles of Riyune's blood flowed out from where the door had been wounded. The shape his body formed wasn't a dog's body, but it wasn't a snake's scale either. It looked more like a cloud waiting patiently for more to gather so it could bring the rain.

The sky above them suddenly cleared. Evening had gathered, with brilliant oranges and purples to the west, over the shank of the spear. Stars appeared. They danced in the darkening heavens before they started flowing.

Away from this place. Back the way Nadeem and Trulliç had

first come.

They could go back now. The desert heart was safe again. Not only was the guard stone safe, it had its own guard dog now.

EPILOGUE

TRULLIÇ

TRULLIÇ LAY UNSLEEPING IN THE cool cavern. He had no idea how long he and Nadeem had walked across the desert, the stars showing them the way, the sand and the winds blowing them along. It hadn't felt as though it had taken as long, though.

Was this place another incarnation of the cavern that held the desert heart? Or was it one and the same place? Had it felt Forit's great need and sacrificed part of itself to her?

Trulliç truly didn't know. He suspected none of the great poems or stories even hinted at such a thing.

Nadeem lay on the shelf above him. They hadn't talked much during their walk. He wasn't sure what to say.

How did he feel about her? He wasn't sure if it was love. The great sage Borceli had declared love would lift his heart like a feather and swirl it on the winds. But that wasn't quite how he felt.

Instead, it was more like she was a part of his heart, like the desert and the night winds. That killing her would have broken him completely.

Or maybe he was already broken. Because he would have killed her if that had meant saving the world.

If he'd had to kill her, he also knew that after he'd dealt with the emperor, he would have joined her in Barzhat's golden court. There would have been nothing left for him to live for.

Not even the desert winds.

Why had Riyune sacrificed himself? Was it so that Trulliç wouldn't have to kill Nadeem? That didn't make sense. Trulliç didn't think that Riyune liked Nadeem all that much.

Nadeem had seen too much of Riyune's true nature, Trulliç felt certain.

He sighed and tried to make himself more comfortable on the cold stone shelf. The small creek beside him burbled now and again. Outside, he knew the stars still raced across the sky, heedless of what went on below.

A soft sound made Trulliç stiffen. He looked over toward the guard stone.

A white shape nosed its way into the small cavern.

Trulliç gasped.

He heard Nadeem gasp as well, obviously awake.

It looked like Riyune. It had that same white and black-spotted fur, the long snout and thin tail.

He could also see *through* the figure, to the bones.

Riyune had returned as a ghost.

The dog didn't appear to notice the difference. He turned three times on the far side of the stream, as if smoothing the ground for his bed. He flopped down, resting his muzzle on his paws. He gave a great yawn, then closed his eyes.

Trulliç could still see *through* the dog. He was but wasn't there.

When Trulliç looked up, he saw Nadeem's head poking over her sleeping shelf. Her huge eyes held questions he couldn't answer. He merely shrugged.

Would the dog still be there in the morning? Would he be a real dog by then?

What was Riyune? What had happened out there on the desert plain?

And what would the emperor do now?

For now, Trulliç could only sleep and hope his dreams held at least some of the answers he needed.

GODS AND GODDESSES

Barzhat

The goddess of death lives beneath the great inner sea of the Tanesh empire. She sits in judgment of the dead on her throne encrusted with pearls and shells. In front of her is a huge golden court, full of souls dancing.

Every bad deed a person commits while they are living is weighed by Barzhat after they die. She creates a black vest covered with golden weights, each shaped like a teardrop. You must dance before Barzhat until all the weights fall from the vest. Only then will Barzhat give you the final kiss of true death, cleansing your soul for rebirth.

A common curse: May you dance forever in the goddess' court.

The star sister Manisat picked up an *ağrikat* shell on the shore of the Barzhat Sea. When she raised the shell to her ear, she heard the sad sighs of the goddess Barzhat and realized how lonely the goddess was. Manisat had made her way to the goddess' golden court while she'd still been alive and had promised the goddess that the star sisters wouldn't merely venerate her, but love her. They would welcome the goddess at all their feasts, big and small. A bowl was always left empty at every meal, a welcome place for the goddess.

Barzhat tests the sisters sometimes, coming for dinner as a stranger.

They must show her hospitality or she will make them dance. However, in return for a star sister's devotion, Barzhat will grant her a single boon during her lifetime, if her need is great enough.

Though cutting across the Barzhat Sea would make travel from one end of the empire to the other faster, no one sails across it regularly. Men can only travel on the waters at her indulgence. Sailors must always be on the lookout when in her territory. If the waters are clear and blue, they can travel freely. If the waters turn black, they run. Otherwise, the goddess takes them down into her golden court where they must dance for centuries.

The goddess is always depicted with two faces, one blue and one black. The blue face is used for judgment. The black face is used for death. She is often called fickle, and is temperamental, as are all artists. She is often shown with four dancing legs and twelve arms, each holding a different weapon.

Symbol: Feet. Also represented by a single line toward the bottom of the space, ___

Colors: Blue and Black.

Innis

The god of fertility lives in the court of the gods. He is forever mourning his beautiful wife, Forist, whom he killed in the great battle with the darkness, and from whom all humanity came. He is known as a dark, somber god. Brining a new life into the world isn't to be done lightly.

Symbol: The spear. Represented by a single horizontal line —

Colors: Red

Serrat/Serril

The goddess/god of desolate places lives in the desert.

Like Barzhat, Serrat/Serril has two faces, a female and a male face. The male aspect (Serril) is worshiped by the land magicians, while the female aspect (Serrat) is honored by the star sisters.

Serrat/Serril is known as a trickster god. He/she leads men and caravans astray in the desert by creating fake oases. He/she also tricks sailors by making Barzhat's waters seem calm.

Yet, Serrat/Serril just wants to be loved.

Originally, Serrat/Serril lived in the court of the gods. However, the gods banished the god/goddess after he brought magic to man. Serril, in his male form, made a bet with the goddess Onnet, that a mighty human hunter could out shoot the goddess and her bow. In order for the hunter to win, Serril gave the human magic.

As Serrat, the goddess has a birthmark in the form of a star on her left cheek, which is why the star sisters carve one in theirs. However, she isn't much loved by them. (They love Berzhat instead.)

Symbol: Z

Colors: White (for Serrat) and black (for Serril)

Enkat

The goddess of rain lives in the court of the gods. She dances for the gods and goddess until the sweat pours from her and drips down from her hair to the earth as rain.

In the desert lands, Enkat is often portrayed as a female form with no face, just hair streaming down everywhere.

Symbol: Represented by three vertical lines. | | |

Colors: Brown and green

Xannil

The god of the sun lives in the court of the gods. In the north, Xannil is often portrayed as a fair-haired, happy god. In the south, he's shown as a darker, sullen, sadistic god. He is married to Enket. Stories tell of how jealous he gets. When he's in a rage, he hides her or sends her away so there's no rain. In addition, Xannil is also jealous of Enket's brother, Innis, the god of fertility. They are forever trying to best each other in drinking contests and wrestling matches, often with disastrous results. Serrat/Serril is usually called to come and fix whatever has been broken.

Symbol: Three horizontal lines.

Color: Yellow

Onnet

The goddess of childbirth and the hunt lives in the court of the gods, though she is often away, traveling, hunting.

Onnet is often portrayed as a crone, though she can take the form of a golden goddess as well. She aids women in childbirth and through their pregnancy. She has a magical bow and can shoot down any prey, no matter how far away. She also uses her bow and magical arrows to bring couples together. There are many stories of young men and women who are great hunters and shoot an arrow into the air, vowing to marry the person who finds it, who after many trials does turn out to be their one true love.

Symbol: Omega. Often represented by a horseshoe.

Color: Orange and green

Creation Myth

In the beginning, there were just the gods and goddesses and no light. Darkness reached everywhere. The gods and goddesses fought with each other all the time just to bring some sort of activity to their endless nights.

So Xannil, the god of the sun, created the first light, which the darkness stole away. He created a second light, which the darkness stole again.

After the third light had been stolen, the gods declared war against the darkness. The darkness divided itself into many beings to fight the gods. The battles raged across the heavens for eons.

Forit, Innis' wife and the fairest of the gods, sang such a beautiful song that the darkness revealed its heart. Innis pierced the heart with his great spear, killing the darkness.

However, the only way Forit could draw out the heart of the darkness was by binding it with her own. When Innis killed the heart of the darkness, he killed his own wife as well.

Forit's body fell from the court of the gods and became the earth. Her teeth became the mountains, her fingers became the many rivers, and the place where her heart had been became the desert.

As the gods and goddesses grieved the loss of the fairest of them all, their tears fell on her prone body.

Forit's freckles, the only imperfection about her, became humanity. The darker freckles became the people of the south, the lighter blemishes became the people of the north.

There are some myths that her heart, still bound with the heart of darkness, lives in the center of the desert.

ABOUT THE AUTHOR

Leah Cutter writes page-turning, wildly imaginative fiction in exotic locations, such as a magical New Orleans, the ancient Orient, Hungary, the Oregon coast, rural Kentucky, Seattle, Minneapolis, and many others.

She writes literary, fantasy, mystery, science fiction, and horror fiction. Her short fiction has been published in magazines like *Alfred Hitchcock's Mystery Magazine* and *Talebones*, anthologies like *Fiction River*, and on the web. Her long fiction has been published both by New York publishers as well as small presses.

Find Leah's books here.
Follow her blog at www.LeahCutter.com.

Come someplace new…

If you'd like to be notified of new releases, sign up for my newsletter.

I will never spam you or use your email for nefarious purposes. You can also unsubscribe at any time.

http://www.LeahCutter.com/newsletter/

Reviews

It's true. Reviews help me sell more books. If you've enjoyed this story, please consider leaving a review of it on your favorite site.

ABOUT KNOTTED ROAD PRESS

Knotted Road Press fiction specializes in dynamic writing set in mysterious, exotic locations.

Knotted Road Press non-fiction publishes autobiographies, business books, cookbooks, and how-to books with unique voices.

Knotted Road Press creates DRM-free ebooks as well as high-quality print books for readers around the world.

With authors in a variety of genres including literary, poetry, mystery, fantasy, and science fiction, Knotted Road Press has something for everyone.

Knotted Road Press
www.KnottedRoadPress.com